SO THE WIND WON'T BLOW IT ALL AWAY

RICHARD BRAUTIGAN was born in Tacoma, Washington where he spent much of his youth, before moving to San Francisco where he became involved with other writers in the Beat Movement. During the Sixties he became one of the most prolific and prominent members of the counter-cultural movement, and wrote some of his most famous novels, including *Trout Fishing in America*, *Sombrero Fallout* and *A Confederate General from Big Sur*.

He was found dead in 1984, aged 49, beside a bottle of alcohol and a .44 calibre gun.

SO THE WIND WON'T BLOW IT ALL AWAY

Richard Brautigan

Introduced by Jeffrey Lent

CANONGATE
Edinburgh · London

First published in the United States of America
in 1982 by Houghton Mifflin Company

This edition published in Great Britain in 2001 by
Rebel Inc, an imprint of
Canongate Books Ltd, 14 High Street,
Edinburgh EH1 1TE

British Library Cataloguing-in-Publication Data
A catalogue record for this book is available on
request from the British Library

ISBN 978 1 84195 075 4

Typeset by Palimpsest Book Production Limited,
Falkirk, Stirlingshire

Printed and bound in Great Britain
by Clays Ltd, St Ives plc

www.canongate.tv

This book is for
Portia Crockett
and Marian Renken.

Introduction: The Longest Wind

ATTEMPTING TO DESCRIBE or categorise the work of Richard Brautigan is strikingly similar to loading mercury with a pitchfork. The most obvious question is what exactly are we trying to fill with the mercury? His early novels were lauded by the critics, later works were panned, as both the critics and the popular audience he achieved confused him with being something called 'the voice of the counterculture'. His final works were largely ignored by all. Even today, many of the Brautigan fans seem to get much of it wrong. Whimsical is the term most often applied and while there are countless ways to describe the work, whimsy is probably the furthest from the mark. This confusion arises no doubt from his striking command of metaphor and his often sly but always somber sense of humor. The vessel of course that we're trying to fill is that shape-changer called reputation. Almost twenty years after his death we're still trying to place this remarkable writer in some category but he deftly slips from grasp just when he seems within reach. Perhaps it would not hurt to recall that mercury is not only hopelessly fluid but poisonous as well.

In my early teens I was living in western New York State, an area predominantly agricultural and about as far as you could get from the cultural upheavals that had and still were occurring. The local public library, while small, nevertheless had one wall of shelves devoted to 'New Titles'. It was here I first discovered the work of contemporary writers such as Charles Portis, Robert Stone, Jim Harrison and Richard

Brautigan. These works struck me with the force of meteors. I still read and look forward to new works by all of these writers, except of course Brautigan, who removed himself from that possibility in 1984 with a gunshot to the head. The last novel published before his death was *So the Wind Won't Blow It All Away*. I was fortunate in being able to read it without the foreknowledge of that suicide. It struck me at the time, and still does today, as being the opening of a new phase in Brautigan's writing. Unfortunately, in an odd way, he seems to have agreed with me, although we obviously reached differing opinions as to what that phase might consist of.

The following lines were written in the fall and winter of 1984–5, following word of his death. Sixteen years later they still come the closest to articulating my reaction and thus the impact his work had upon me. Certainly an imperfect poem, it remains what I have to offer to the spirit of an incomparable man of letters and his lovely, wrenching language.

Late last summer, early last fall
the news came through as a single flat statement.
It was weeks as bits trickled in so some skewed picture
    emerged
although that first week NPR ran a profile and
    reiterated
what we'd all heard before and so knew to be true
of this minor writer and voice of the flower children –
Like natives naked dancing hotfoot about the torn and
    dismembered
body of the white hunter, digging in spear points to
    partake and obliterate
any mystery he'd ceased to hold.

It was true.
At least it seemed that way until finally you agreed.
Now of course we're freed to question those
    pronouncements.

You died in a gunfight, the walls diving behind bottles
in a vain attempt to escape your deadly hand.
But you showed no mercy least of all to yourself
though more than once I imagine you lifting the barrel
    after the barrage,
placing it hot against the side of your nose
to view the dead over your own sizzling skin
(that fisherman knowledge of lubricating ferrules on the
    nose-tip).
A photograph shows you kneeling in waders on a grass-
    smooth riverbank,
hair leonine and the ten-speed handlebar moustache swept
    back. You hold a rod
and there is a young boy standing before you. What did
    you teach him, Richard?
To tie nail knots, blood knots, how to cast, how to stand
    in waist deep current?
How to read water?
Someone perhaps the boy's father, said,
Things just won't be fun witout Richard anymore.
I suspect otherwise.
Are you now night air that lies over the Yellowstone, the
    Madison, Nelson Spring Creek,
trout leaping from the water into you and in release
    back again?

Do you no longer bother with whiskey?

If in anger or sadness you gave up young women
long ago

I hope you find them again, running unseen through
their clothes

and springing off with laughter and warmth.

A group of your friends offered up for national
publication remembrances

reading like a list of sad songs and righteousness.

You never should have lived there but you did. Thirty
miles

from town a man who would not drive a car.

We are always unprepared for the moments of the day.

Air becomes pain.

I didn't know you. Our eyes never met.

This is a letter to the dead as a younger brother writes
to a soldier in a distant land,

a younger brother who hasn't seen war but dreams the
filth of bloodshed every night.

By your own hand.

You were always, as the best are, so very visible but
something odd happened along the way.

Through your own choice or not you became the elephant
foot umbrella stand,

the bowling trophies, the rusted machinery, the wheel-
chair.

Venereal warts and no silk ribboned sombrero.

You always liked those big hats but in the end they ceased
belonging to you.

They continue to bust the grateful dead and a very few
very old women

continue to receive Confederate veteran benefits but
no-one cares.
Libraries are strictly controlled and you must provide
ample proof of residency.
If you ever had that to begin with
it's gone now.

Last night I spoke with a friend about the immediacy of
anger deployed successfully,
that great need. But when you're the only one there what
is the use?
The month you spent decomposing on the floor surely
you learned something.
The phone ringing, the messages unanswered on the
machine.
All those nights last summer I spent trying to call Jim
or John or Allison
I might better have called you. But you seemed so far
from reach
and I need the uplifting tune myself. It seems now you
had lost yourself
for so many years and were only awaiting a moment
and on that point let's keep clear —
One voice one word one thought can't hold it back.
What was the tool? I'm curious.
I consider the coroners report but that's only one man's
tired opinion
and we both know what the weapon really was.
It had all left and that finally is enough.
I like to think if you'd had crops to tend or stock to
watch or even a bitch in heat

that might've done the trick. The notions of a child.

All that was there were shadows and as so seen worse
   at night.

There are more than enough cruel words for us all and
   little enough of

encouragement and grown men that we are these things
   are vital. More so

are the silences that must be endured and the words
   stretching off into the dark

just when it seems someone must speak.

The shadows are our dearest friends even if they chew
   at our legs like puppies trying new teeth.

But that was forgotten or lost or no. No for the shadow
   became the closest friend that

reached and touched, stroked, and finally owned.

Ray Bergman wrote, 'One word of caution if you wish
   to calibrate your own gut.

Gut bruises easily and when bruised it is really worse
   than broken because it is deceptive,

not noticeable yet weak.' He speaks of leaders which are
   nothing more than threads on which

life is strung. Some of us do this several times a day and
   most grow accustomed but

in some houses children and wives are routinely beaten,
   dogs kicked.

We become automations that produce or don't. I, myself,
   have carried old appliances

to the dump.

Old ones are stacked in homes and visited the day after

Christmas before we hurry away.

I don't want those sad words anymore than do you. Lock them up

if they're not gracious enough to turn their own key. We are hurt

by loved ones and then can lay blame.

Abandoned by wives, children, parents we are mercifully free to lay blame.

We are the perfect hope if it weren't for them.

We legitimize our failure to send child support or the kids for the promised Easter break.

In a just world we would be lined up against the wall.

In this world we may have the rather distinct pleasure of lining ourselves up.

If you wish to calibrate your own gut the first tool needed is a razor.

To gather this takes nothing more than courage though we generally call it the other.

No matter. You lay like a squashed rabbit or more truly a skunk on the road for weeks.

In the heat of mid-afternoon we thought we could smell something.

Stagnant water. The pail in the corner of the abortion clinic.

Horsepiss on dust.

One friend said O yes I remember him all the young girls used to read him.

That certainly seemed to sum it up. Another said I haven't heard that name in years,

I didn't think anyone else read him but I've got his last

book right here and you say

he shot himself? One of these two have read reviews and
forgotten how to think.

Oh Richard these are perfect poems, perfect vignettes,
perfect novels. This is it.

Let this be my final judgement.

Let us admit Sheep that once again we have missed the
train at the station and now

Watch only its smoke across the far edge of the plain.

Oh Richard tonight it's late and I weep for you as for
my father,

the both of you lost down that cyclone of silent self.

I can never know the guts of the details but am trying
to understand that final statement.

The rest is detail but this is the dark.

You can't claim oppression of fatigue.

Neither failure or misunderstanding.

This ain't that kind of deal.

You should have known that long enough to have gotten
used to the idea.

I'm angry because you wouldn't keep going.

Long before you seriously sign up you know what the
odds are.

    One of the rocks on my desk is from the coast of
      Maine, another is a coral chunk from the Keys.

    There are small polished dull blue pebbles from Lake
      Michigan.

    It might not be much from an emotional point of view
      but the planet is all we really have.

    Somehow the Maine rock has traveled with me
      thousands of miles, the coral also.

Time to time I hold one or the other against my lips
and think of water.
The blue rocks are in a pouch, holy dice from the
water of love,
The earth of fire and the sky of perpetual building
rain.
Rain that becomes, always, rain.

Shortly before noon I realized that if a conclusion is to
be reached it must be grasped.
This has been one long circling of a thicket in the dark.
Inside the tight-grown branches
and stalks there rests something, Perhaps it's myself.
Perhaps not.
Perhaps I've dwelt overmuch on your death.
All men come to the same end — it's the everything leading
up that's of import.
Still the taboo of suicide remains. We remain. We remain
and that seems the
most cardinal of dictum. Each man suffers according to
his own ability.
This is simple stuff but to understand the simplicity of
that abrasive diffusion of
brain requires stripping away to some essential level.
Notice that I reject accident.
In these matters there is no accidental function.
Lead itself is a plastic but inelastic substance. Had you
been this angry since birth?
I hope you were clear-eyed and your hand was steady.
I suspect you'd been drunk since dawn and needing to
cry for several days.

In the end all of this doesn't matter and you are removed
from us now.
That is was your choice and not a ravage of cancer,
a youth loose with a car as you shambled along the road
with the stars on your shoulders,
that your finger circled the trigger and not some coked-up
sport from Chicago
mistaking your form for a bull elk,
the trout stream, the one you always went to alone
. . . all of these things don't, finally, matter. Your being
is gone.
Talk of history or future or fate if futile, a hand-job of
the mind.
A freak August freeze has blackened more than a few
tomato plants,
fruit split, broken on the ground.

Tonight I listen to old recordings of western swing after
another day following my
mind along like a tired hound jogging behind the two
high rear wheels of a westbound stage,
the crack of the whip over the horses no longer plunging
me forward in a short burst
but steady dog-trotting.
There is enough ecstasy in the music to uplift me
tonight.
This won't always happen but I do know it wouldn't
happen if I wasn't looking for it.
If I found it everytime it wouldn't be enough either.
The rear wheels raise a fine constant filter of dust,
shielding the dog from sight of everything

until the stage rattles over a shallow streambed and
up a rise.
The wind blows into Montana all the way from California.
The dog stops to drink.

So The Wind Won't Blow It All Away
Dust ... American ... Dust

Jeffrey Lent
December 2000

So the Wind Won't Blow it All Away

I DIDN'T KNOW that afternoon that the ground was waiting to become another grave in just a few short days. Too bad I couldn't grab the bullet out of the air and put it back into the .22 rifle barrel and have it spiral itself back down the barrel and into the chamber and refasten itself to the shell and be as if it had never been fired or even loaded into the gun.

I wish the bullet was back in its box with the other 49 brother and sister bullets and the box was safely on the shelf in the gunshop, and I had just walked by the shop on that rainy February afternoon and never gone inside.

I wish I had been hungry for a hamburger instead of bullets. There was a restaurant right next to the gunshop. They had very good hamburgers, but I wasn't hungry.

For the rest of my life I'll think about that hamburger. I'll be sitting there at the counter, holding it in my hands with tears streaming down my cheeks. The waitress will be looking away because she doesn't like to see kids crying when they are eating hamburgers, and also she doesn't want to embarrass me.

I am the only customer in the restaurant.

She doesn't need this.

She has her own problems.

Her boyfriend left her last week for a redhead from Chicago. This is the second time in a year this has happened to her. She can't believe it. It has to be more than a coincidence. How many redheads are there in Chicago?

She takes a rag and cleans up an imaginary stain far down

the counter, wiping up something spilled that isn't there. I'll continue on with this story:

So the Wind Won't Blow It All Away
Dust . . . American . . . Dust

It was the second year after World War II ended, when they rattled down a rutted, mud-hardened road toward the pond in an old pickup truck that had their fishing furniture piled on the back. It was always around 7 o'clock in the summer evenings of 1947 when they pulled up beside the pond and began taking their furniture off the truck.

First, they took the couch off. It was a big heavy couch but it was no problem for them because they were both big heavy people. She was just about as big as he was. They put the couch down on the grass right beside the pond, so they could sit there and fish off the couch.

They always took the couch off first and then they got the rest of the furniture. It took them no time at all to set up their things. They were very efficient at it and obviously had been doing this for years before I saw them and began waiting for them to arrive at the pond and became, in my own small way, a part of their life.

Sometimes I would arrive early and wait for them.

As I sit here on August 1st, 1979, my ear is pressed up against the past as if to the wall of a house that no longer exists.

I can hear the sound of redwing blackbirds and the wind blowing hard against the cattails. They rustle in the wind like ghost swords in battle and there is the steady lapping of the pond at the shore's edge, which I belong to with my imagination.

The blackbirds sound like melancholy exclamation marks typed on the summer late afternoon, which has a feeling of bored exhaustion because a hot wind is blowing from the south. That kind of wind is always tiring and gets on my nerves.

A plank has been crudely engineered with the help of a small log at the end and some stake-like pilings to form at best the world's saddest fishing dock.

It's really pathetic, and all of my own design and construction, so there's really no one else to blame, and I'm standing on the end of it, about twelve feet away from the shore. The plank cuts a narrow corridor through the cattails to get to the open water of the pond. The plank sags in the middle, so it's covered with three inches of water, and it's not solid enough to jump over.

My clown-like dock would collapse if I tried that, so I have to wade through the water to get to the dry end of the plank to fish.

Fortunately, twelve-year-old boys don't care if they get their tennis shoes wet. It means practically nothing to them. They couldn't care less, so I'm standing there with wet feet, fishing into the southern wind, listening to the blackbirds and the dry sword-like rustling of the cattails and the steady lapping of the water against where the pond ends and the shore of the world begins.

I'm fishing directly across the pond from where they will come in a few hours and set up their furniture.

I'm waiting for them by watching my bobber bobbing up and down like a strange floating metronome and slowly drowning a worm because the fish are not interested in the slightest with its plight.

The fish just aren't biting, but I don't care.

I'm just waiting and this is as good a way to wait as any other way to wait because waiting's all the same anywait.

The sun is shining on the water in front of me, so I have to keep looking away. Whenever I look at the sun, it is reflected back to me like a shiny bedspread whose design is hundreds of wind-driven roller coasters.

There is no freshness to the sun.

The sun turned boring in the middle of the afternoon, as it does so often for children, and was almost out of style like old clothes that were poorly and uninterestingly designed from the very beginning. Maybe He should have thought twice about it.

The sun was burning me slightly but I didn't care. My face felt a little flushed. I wasn't wearing a hat. I seldom wore hats when I was a child. Hats were to come later on.

I had almost albino white hair.

Kids called me 'Whitey.'

I had been standing there so long that my tennis shoes were almost dry. They were at their half-life, which is the best time for tennis shoes. They felt as if they were truly a part of me like an extension of my soles. They were alive at the bottoms of my feet.

I didn't like it when my tennis shoes completely wore out and we didn't have any money to buy another pair. I always felt as if I had done something bad and was being punished for it.

I must be a better kid!

This was how God was punishing me: by making me wear

fucked-up old tennis shoes, so that I was embarrassed to look at my own feet.

I was too young and naive then to link up the meaning of those ridiculingly defunct tennis shoes that I was forced to wear with the reality that we were on Welfare and Welfare was not designed to provide a child with any pride in its existence.

When I got a new pair of tennis shoes, my outlook on life immediately changed. I was a new person and proud to walk on the earth again and thanked God in my prayers for helping me get a new pair of tennis shoes.

But in the meantime it was the summer of 1947, and I got bored waiting for them to come with their furniture and decided to go visit an old man who was a night watchman at a small sawmill nearby.

He lived in a little shack by the sawmill and drank beer. He drank a lot of beer while he watched the sawmill, so that no one took anything. The sawmill was very, very quiet after the workers went home. He watched it with a bottle of beer in his hand. I think you could have stolen the entire sawmill and he wouldn't have noticed it.

I would often visit him and he would give me his empty beer bottles and I would return them to the store and get a penny apiece deposit for them.

Collecting his beer bottles was a good idea.

It beat looking into the sun.

I waded back across the plank and my feet were wet again. It took only a few seconds to make it as if they had never been dry, that they had always been wet, but I didn't care.

I had to make the decision whether to take my bamboo fishing pole with me because there was a place along the way where I sometimes jigged for frogs or hide it in the bushes. I stood there and took about ten seconds longer to make that decision than I should have.

I hid my pole in some bushes.

The idea of frogs was as boring as the sun.

I would pick it up when I came back to join the man and the woman in their open fishing house across the pond. I was now ahead of them in time, so I would give them a couple of hours to catch up.

There were other things that I could do besides not catch fish until they came and the night watchman's beer bottles was one of them.

While I walked a quarter of a mile to the sawmill, my mind was occupied with fantasies of empty beer bottles. Maybe he had two cases of them or perhaps even three. I hadn't visited him in a week or so and maybe he had been drinking more beer than usual. I hoped that was the case. Then I had the sobering thought that maybe another kid had already visited him and gotten all the beer bottles that should rightfully have been mine.

I didn't like the idea of that kid.

I vowed to make it a regular part of my life to visit that old man at least every four days and get all of his beer bottles for myself.

The loss of that revenue was no laughing matter, especially if part of your life you had to wear shitty tennis shoes.

During those years just after World War II, I could be quite a formidable collector of beer bottles if I put my mind to it. They were worth a penny apiece for the small ones and two cents apiece for quarts.

When I was in a very serious beer-bottle mood, I would take an old baby buggy with me. It was made out of wicker and had a huge hood. I could put a lot of beer bottles in that buggy.

Sometimes I would spend a whole day pushing it around, collecting abandoned beer bottles. Within a mile of where we lived, there were many opportunities for a young beer-bottle capitalist if he pushed his baby buggy hard and long enough.

There was a highway to be explored. People liked to drink beer in their cars and throw the bottles out the windows where they would land in my baby buggy a week later.

The highway stretched between cities and went all the way across the state, but I used only a mile of it as part of my beer-bottle empire.

That mile was on the edge of town where I lived with my mother and two sisters in a cabin at an auto court, but we didn't have an automobile. We never had one. We were autoless guests of the Welfare Department. It was strange all those people coming and going to and from different places when we were going nowhere.

My mother and my sisters won't be mentioned again because they are not really a part of this story. That of course is a lie. They will be mentioned later on. I don't know why I just told this lie. It was really a silly and useless thing for me to do, but sometimes people do silly and useless things. They can't help themselves. They are often at the mercy of unknown vectors.

I have corrected it, though, and now we can continue on without, I hope, too much loss of credibility, and please remember that I could have changed this story to cover my lie and *actually* have left them out and substituted an aunt and two cousins in their place.

So please accept my apology and be prepared for them to reappear on page 10.

The highway went right past the auto court and I followed it out of town with my baby buggy. I got the baby buggy from an old woman who said she'd give me something if I went to the store for her. I said OK, and she gave me a list of things she wanted and the money to pay for them.

'Can I trust you?' she said, pausing a very old hand on the clasp of an equally old black leather purse.

'Yes,' I said, already holding the list in my hand. We had already gone that far with the deal, so she was holding onto the last flickering doubts of an already negotiated deal. All I needed was the money. We were both very aware of this. She sighed and opened the purse at the same time, saying, 'I wish my husband wasn't dead.'

'What did he die of?' I said, not really caring but knowing that I had to say something. You can't leave a remark like that alone without an attending comment, or so I thought at the time.

'A heart attack. He died in bed. He was an older man.'

She handed me two dollars.

'When?' I chirped like a little death sparrow.

The money was old and crumpled like the woman. She must have had it for a very long time. Maybe she slept on it while dreaming of her dead husband. Old people are supposed to do that: sleep on their money, snoring on top of thousands of George Washingtons and Abraham Lincolns.

'March 3, 1916.'

I did some primitive arithmetic in my mind which has not been too good at arithmetic, anyway, and then said, 'He's been dead for a long time.'

'Too long,' she said. 'I can hardly remember what it was like.'

I didn't know the full meaning of what she was saying.

I do now.

When I came back with the sack of groceries, she gave me the baby buggy. It was in a garage full of other old things right beside the weather-worn house that she lived in. The paint had fallen off the house years before, so the house just stood there in the neighborhood, hardly noticed any more.

The garage was very complicated in the light of a 15 watt globe fastened to a piece of yellow string that looked as if it had come off a mummy.

There were many perfectly packed boxes of the past in the garage and there were hundreds of things that were mostly shadows. Its reality was only the memories now of children grown up and away from the buggy.

'I think you can just wheel it out,' she said.

I walked very carefully over to the baby buggy. I didn't want to stumble over the past and break my present-tense leg that might leave me crippled in the future.

I took the handle of the baby buggy and pulled it away from the 1900s and into the year 1947.

Though I was in the garage for just a short time, when I emerged pushing the baby buggy, the afternoon seemed extraordinarily bright. It was a cloudy day but it seemed as if the sun were out and shining in full magnitude.

I helped her close the garage door. She was just about too old to do it by herself. I guess when she got too old to close the garage door, she'd go live in an old folks home with other people who were too old to close their garage doors.

She padlocked the door with a very ancient and fragile lock. The lock was only a symbol of privacy and protection, but that meant something in those days. If that lock were around today, a thief would just walk up to it and blow it off with his breath.

'Do you want me to come back and do some more errands for you?' I said.

'No,' she said.

I shrugged my shoulders and pushed the baby buggy away into my life where I pretended that it was a covered wagon for a while and pulled my sisters* and other kids around in it. I pretended that I was at the head of a wagon train of baby buggies crossing the Great Plains going West in the pioneer days to homestead Oregon.

There were many perils to be overcome: hostile Indians, the burning sun and lack of water, and also sudden unexplainable snowstorms that we got lost in and had to find the trail all over again.

After a week the romantic possibilities of babybuggy pioneer days wore out my imagination and I changed it into a beer-bottle carrier.

The baby buggy gave me a tremendous ease of mobility and the chance, because of its capacity, to become a beer-bottle millionaire.

Before I got the buggy, I used gunnysacks to transport the bottles. Now with the baby buggy, I was breathing on the neck of John D. Rockefeller.

Maybe I was thinking about that as I walked over to the sawmill to investigate the night watchman's capacity for beer drinking and how it could help me see a John Wayne movie or experince the awkward joy of trying to keep one lick ahead

*I kept my word. See page 7.

of an ice-cream cone on a hot summer day. Shitty tennis shoes were not a problem at this time.

In the area just around the pond where the people came in the evening and set up their furniture, there were two other ponds and half-a-dozen sawmills with their accompanying log ponds.

The center of the area was an overpass on the highway.

Underneath the overpass travelling north and south was a railroad line that the sawmills used to supply America with houses. Coal-burning trains were constantly coming and going along the tracks. I used to pretend that pieces of coal that fell off the tenders were gigantic black diamonds and I was the richest kid in the world and bought everything a child could use or imagine with the coal that fell off the passing trains.

Besides the sawmill activities that went on in the area, there were also open fields and some agricultural lands with livestock: horses and cows and sheep. There were two previously planted and domesticated orchards that had been totally ignored, abandoned for reasons unknown and had reverted to the wild, bearing apples and pears and plums and cherries that had a tremendous amount of character. They made the fruit that you bought in the store seem like a bunch of sissies.

All of this started when I opened the front door of the auto court cabin where I lived and I never got to explore all of it because it just kept unfolding new territories until my childhood ended when I was twelve years old on February 17th, 1948, in yet another abandoned orchard five miles away in the opposite direction where I was always headed, though I did not know it at the time.

But now it was still the summer of 1947 and I cut over from the pond to the railroad tracks and walked north along the tracks toward the possible beer-bottle riches of a used-up old man who watched a sawmill at night, so nobody would drive carefully up in a truck with its lights out and steal the saw which would cause a lot of commotion when the mill hands came to work the next morning.

'Where's the saw?'

There were three sawmills north of the overpass along the tracks and the night watchman's was the last sawmill. It was just past quitting time when I arrived there. He had a shack to the side of the mill. There were a hell-of-a-lot of tall weeds growing around the shack. There were millions of weeds in that area, but these weeds were so tall that they attracted attention where normally that would not have happened. They would have just been another patch of weeds and gone very unnoticed.

The old man was sitting on the front porch of the shack surrounded by his weeds. He had a bottle of beer in his hand. That was a good sign. There was an empty bottle lying on its side next to the chair he was sitting in. That was even a better sign. The old man didn't know that as I walked toward him all I really saw was two cents.

'Hello, kid,' he said. 'Come to pay me a little visit?'

The dry gray chair he was sitting in looked just like another weed. Sometimes I thought about that. I wondered if it was possible to make a chair out of weeds. If they had ever made one, he was sitting in it.

'Yes, sir,' I said.

'Nineteen empties,' he said.

'What?' I said.

'You've got that empty-beer-bottle look in your eyes,' the old man said and then repeated, 'Nineteen empties.'

'Oh,' I said, looking down at the ground that somehow

seemed very far away. I didn't know that it was that obvious. I wondered what I could do about it and then realized that there was nothing I could do about it. It was the truth and would always be the truth, so I looked up from the distant ground.

'Nice day,' I said, trying hard to assert my twelve-year-old personality.

'They're on the back porch in a gunnysack,' he said. 'Why don't you get them while I take a real good look at this nice day of yours. Just go right through the house and I'll tell you what I think when you get back.'

'Thank you,' I said.

'Don't thank me,' he said. 'Just thank the fact that I'm an alcoholic.'

I knew that did not need a reply, so I walked up the five weed-attacked steps to the front porch where the old man was sitting in a chair that the weeds had already conquered, with a bottle of beer in his hand which he very carefully drew to his mouth to take a sip. Rembrandt could not have drawn a more direct or finer line.

Before I open the screen door and go into the shack I'd like to make an observation. I keep referring to the sawmill night watchman alcoholic as an 'old man.' But looking back down upon that long-ago past now from the 1979 mountainside of this August afternoon, I think the 'old man' was younger than I am now. He was about maybe thirty-five, nine years younger than I am now. To the marshy level of my human experience back then, he seemed to be very old, probably the equivalent of an eighty-year-old man to me now.

Also, drinking beer all the time didn't make him look any younger.

I knew very little about him. I knew that somehow he had

gotten out of the Army and had spent the rest of the War in Mobile, Alabama, where he drank a lot of beer and married a woman who left him after two years of marriage because she didn't want to be around a man who drank so much beer.

She thought that there were better things in life, so she divorced him. He had loved her very much, so the divorce just contributed to him drinking more beer.

Once when he was talking about her to me with his inevitable bottle of beer in hand, I realized that he never spoke of her by name, so I asked him what her name was. He took a very long sip of beer before replying. Then he said after what seemed like an hour to me that her name was not important and to just think of her as the woman who had broken his heart.

I didn't say anything to that either.

I knew that didn't require an answer either.

I opened the screen door and walked into his little one-room shack, which for some strange reason was very tidy. He may have been a drunk but he was neat.

Besides a few sticks of elemental furniture, there were very few personal effects in the shack. A picture of Jesus on the wall seemed out of place, but that was his and His business, not mine. The picture of Jesus was hanging crookedly, so I didn't think that he was much of a Christian.

Maybe the picture of Jesus covered a crack in the wall.

He had some letters on the table. They were always the same two letters. They had both been opened very neatly. One of the letters was from Pensacola, Florida, and it was postmarked September 1, 1939. I guess if he drank as much beer as he did, people didn't write to him that often.

There were no bills on the table.

He had very carefully arranged a lifestyle that denied even the remotest possibility of getting a bill.

I never touched his mail. I wasn't that kind of kid. I mean, of course, I was a sneak, but not that kind of sneak. The imagination was where I snuck around.

I always walked very slowly and close to the table and nonchalantly glanced at his mail. That was as far as I carried it. Another letter was from Little Rock, Arkansas, and it was postmarked April 4, 1942.

It was from a man named Edgar Peters. I wonder why that name still sticks in my mind after all these years. I've forgotten a lot more important things. I've even forgotten things that I don't even know that I knew. They are totally gone, but there's Edgar Peters like a Las Vegas neon sign someplace in my brain.

There was a postcard tacked to the wall beside the kitchen sink which was right next to the back door that always led me to empty beer bottles.

The postcard was extremely intriguing to me and I always eagerly waited to see it again. The contents of the postcard were facing the wall, so I don't know who it was from except that the card was postmarked July 12, 1938, and it was mailed from New Orleans, and the postmark should have been on the other side.

The picture on that postcard probably meant more to me than the existence of that 'old man' other than his capacity to make me money by drinking beer.

It was a color photograph of a flatbed truck with a huge catfish on it that took up the whole bed. The catfish was maybe the size of a whale. Think about Moby Dick to my twelve-year-old way of looking at things and you're very close to the truth. The postcard was some kind of trick photography, but 50% of me believed that it was real.

Once that 50% gained total control of my mind and I asked him if that was a real catfish. Maybe I had spent too much time fishing in the sun that day.

'Are you kidding?' he replied.

'I guess so,' I said. 'How did they do that?'

'I don't know,' he said. 'If I knew how they did that I wouldn't be the night watchman of a half-assed sawmill out in the middle of nowhere.'

No reply from me was forthcoming.

Another thing about him that I was aware of back then and it gave me pause to think, not long but a little, was that all the few personal references to his life had something to do with the South.

He had spent the War in Mobile, Alabama.

He had a catfish postcard from New Orleans.

He had married a Southern woman.

He had one letter from Pensacola, Florida, and another letter from Little Rock, Arkansas.

He had all these things that related him to the South, but he didn't have a Southern accent, not even in the slightest. The sound of his voice was at least a billion miles away from Robert E. Lee.

So I thought about it briefly sometimes, but not that often. If I had something better to think about other than the fact that an 'old' alcoholic sawmill night watchman didn't have a Southern accent, I would think about whatever that was gladly.

I opened the screen door and stepped out onto the back porch into an army of huge weeds that grew over the porch, almost trying to get into the shack and find out why that 'old man' didn't have a Southern accent and maybe even the name of his wife who had left him in 1944 because he drank so much beer and she didn't want to sleep beside another beer fart in the middle of a hot Mobile night with the wind not stirring at all.

I picked up the sack of beer bottles and journeyed back through the house to the 'old man' waiting for me on the front porch with probably something cynical to say about my 'nice day' observation, but I didn't care because I had his beer bottles and I had looked at his catfish postcard and his letter from Edgar Peters, writing to him about something that will always remain a mystery to me. Maybe the contents of the letter told him to stop drinking so much beer all the time or his friends would give up on him.

When I came out the other side of the shack onto the front porch, lugging my beer bottles, he totally surprised me by saying, 'You're right. It is a nice day and you've got nineteen fine beer bottles in that sack. I had a lot more last week. Three cases or so. Too bad you didn't come by then. You'd be rolling in dough.'

He smiled when he said that.

Three cases! I thought.

'Some other kid got them,' he said.

'Who was that?' I said, trying to sound casual while mentally running through a list of kid enemies in my mind. Sometimes other kids got to the 'old man's' beer bottles before I did. Anyone who took his bottles other than myself was not a friend of mine.

It's interesting that the 'old man' never returned any of the bottles himself because I knew that he wasn't rich. I guess he just went to the store and got the beer and brought it back to the sawmill and sat there and drank it and then waited for us kids to come and scavenge the bottles away like empty-beer-bottle hyenas.

'It was some kid you don't know,' he said, lowering my curiosity. 'He lives in the opposite direction from you. I think he lives somewhere near Melody Ranch.'

Melody Ranch was a cheap roadhouse dance hall where there were a lot of fistfights on the weekend between drunken men who would never sit in the chair where Harry Truman was sitting. It was out of my territory, so the kid was an unknown competitor, just another vulture circling the alcoholism of this 'old' night watchman.

I used to wonder what he would do if somebody actually came to the sawmill at night and tried to steal something. He had a thin beer-brittle physique. Some men get fat when they drink a lot of beer. Others just get thinner until their bones come to resemble dried-out weeds. He was that type.

Also, there is something else that I haven't mentioned about him. He was a very fancy dresser and his clothes were immaculately neat and clean.

Sometimes he wore a suit with a tie while he watched the sawmill with a faithful bottle of beer in his hand. He looked like an insurance agent instead of a night watchman. I wondered about his capability and desire to defend the sawmill against sawmill thieves because he looked as if he couldn't defend a marshmallow against a three-year-old.

Perhaps he had a gun.

I asked him about that once.

'What do I need a gun for?' was his reply.

I didn't pursue that subject but finally I had to ask him what he would do if somebody came and tried to steal something.

'I'd let them steal the whole God-damn sawmill. I wouldn't help them load it, though. I wouldn't want to get my clothes dirty. They only pay me fifty dollars a month to watch this God-forsaken place, plus I get to live in this shack for nothing and they take care of my utilities.'

He laughed when he said the words: 'my utilities.' Then he said them again but this time much louder, 'My utilities!' and laughing even louder. I tried to think what was so funny, but I couldn't, so I left.

Anyway, that was a few months ago and this was now and I had a sack of beer bottles and I was ready to go on my way again. I had to get back to the pond.

The people who brought their furniture with them when they went fishing would be arriving soon, and they were much more interesting than this carefully dressed 'old' beer-drinking sawmill night watchman who didn't give a damn if thieves came and took the whole place, mill, pond, logs, lumber, and just left him there drinking beer with everything gone except for his little shack and his weed-like chair on the front porch.

'I have to be going,' I said, taking a step back and away from his world.

'Well, don't go to Mobile, Alabama,' he said, starting to laugh.

My second step was a little more hurried.

'Mobile, Alabama!' he repeated:

So the Wind Won't Blow It All Away
Dust . . . American . . . Dust

The afternoon sun was appropriately lower in the sky and the wind was beginning to die down and there was an advanced feeling of evening approaching with its refreshing contents and renewed hope after a long hot summer afternoon.

While I'm a quarter of a mile away, walking back to the pond with a sack of beer bottles over my shoulder, I'll talk about something else that is more interesting than just walking along various well-worn paths and then railroad tracks leading to a final path ending or perhaps beginning at the pond again.

As a child I was very interested when other children died. There was no doubt about it that I was a morbid kid and when other children died, it always fanned the flames of my forensic curiosity.

Later, in Febraury of 1948, this curiosity would become a personal reality and engulf and turn my life upside down and inside out like *Alice in Wonderland* taking place in a cemetery with the white rabbit as an undertaker and Alice wearing a grave-eaten shroud to play her games in.

But in my life before that was to happen, I was fascinated by dead children and the aftermath of their passing. I think it all perhaps began in 1940 when we moved into an apartment that was annexed to a funeral parlor.

The apartment had once been a functioning part of the mortuary. I don't know exactly what part, but the undertaker to get a little extra cash had changed the former dead space of his funeral parlor into an apartment where we lived for a few months in the late spring of 1940.

I used to get up in the mornings and watch the funerals out the window. I had to stand on a chair because I was five years old and I wanted a good view.

I seem to remember they held some funerals early in the

morning because everybody would still be asleep in the apartment and I would be wearing my pajamas.

To get at the funerals I had to roll up a window shade that was particularly difficult for my dexterity to handle, but somehow I managed it and then pulled a chair over and stood on top of it and watched the funerals.

We moved into the apartment late one afternoon and the next morning while everybody was still asleep, I got up and wandered into the front room. I looked sleepily under the window shade and there was my first funeral as big as death.

The hearse was parked maybe thirty feet away. Can you imagine how big that hearse seemed? That's very close for a hearse to be to a five-year-old. It seemed to me to be the size of a movie that for some very strange reason they had painted black.

That's when I first went and got the chair and pulled the window shade up after quite a struggle and moved the chair into a very good funeral-viewing position and climbed on top of it.

I did this all very quietly because I didn't want to wake anybody up in the house. Adults always like to disrupt what kids are doing, no matter what it is except if it's something the kid doesn't like. If the kid doesn't like it, the adults will let him keep on doing it forever, but if the kid likes it . . .

The hearse was filled with flowers.

There were so many flowers in the hearse that ever since then flowers have always made me feel uneasy. I like flowers but sometimes I feel uncomfortable being in their presence. I've never let it get out of control, but I've had it ever since that morning in 1940 when I watched my first funeral.

For a while the hearse and all its flowers were just standing there alone except for two men dressed in black who seemed not to be in a hurry, just waiting. They could almost have been flowers themselves: some kind of black daffodils.

One of them was smoking a cigarette. He had smoked it down so short that it looked as if the butt were going to set his hand on fire. The other one kept stroking a long very black moustache that looked as if it had jumped off the hearse and right onto his face, but it didn't seem to bother him.

You probably want to know how I knew I was watching a funeral if I was only five years old and I had never seen this sort of thing before and nobody had told me about such goings on. The answer to this is very simple: I saw one in the movies, just a week before and figured it out for myself.

After a while the two men who were waiting beside the hearse went into the funeral parlor and then people started coming out. The people were all very somber and moved appropriately. They seemed to be in slow motion. Though I was close to them, standing on my chair, it was difficult to hear what they were saying.

This was becoming very interesting.

I could hardly wait to see what would happen next.

The two men in black came back out with some other men carrying the coffin. They put it in the back of the hearse. Actually, they had to sort of stuff it in because of all the flowers, but somehow they managed it and the two men got into the front seat where the living travelled.

The mourners walked very *s l o w l y* and started getting into parked cars. The cars all had one-word signs on their windshields, but I didn't know what the word said. It would be years before. I figured it out.

Pretty soon everybody was gone and the street was very

quiet in the wake of their departure. The first thing I heard after they were gone was a bird singing just outside the window.

I got down from the chair and went back to my bed. I lay there staring at the ceiling and digesting what I had just seen. I stayed in bed until everybody else woke up.

When I heard them moving around in the kitchen, I got up and joined them. They were still sleepy and making some coffee to begin the war of another day.

They asked me if I'd had a good night's sleep.

For an unknown reason I pondered their question, which really didn't even need a reply. I mean, I could have said any little thing and that would have been OK, but I stood there, thinking hard about it.

They continued what they were already doing and immediately forgot that they had asked me something. People aren't really interested for any length of time if a five-year-old had a good night's sleep, and that's what was happening to me.

'Yes, I did,' I finally said.

'Did what?' they asked.

'Had a good night's sleep.'

'Oh,' they said, looking at me curiously because they had forgotten what they had asked me. Adults are always doing that with children.

Anyway, I got up early and watched the funerals after that. There of course wasn't a funeral every morning and I was disappointed when there wasn't one. I went back to bed and hoped that there would be a funeral the next morning.

There were other funerals going on during the day but I didn't care about them very much.

I was strictly a morning funeral child.

For the first two weeks I did that, everybody stayed asleep

in the apartment. Then one morning somebody got up early and found me standing on a chair in the front room, with my pajamas on, looking out the window at a funeral.

They came up quietly behind me and looked at what I was watching with total attention, so much so that I didn't even hear them come up.

I must have been a very strange sight.

'What are you doing?' they asked, but they could see what I was doing, so in a way, it was a wasted question.

'Looking out the window,' I said.

'Looking out the window at a funeral. You're a weird kid.'

I have to agree that observation was right on the money.

They said that they wanted to have a serious conversation with me later on, but they forgot about it and so the serious conversation never took place.

The undertaker had a wife and a little daughter. They lived in the funeral parlor along with the dead people. The daughter was a year older than I. She was six and had very cold hands. I guess living in a funeral parlor gave a person cold hands.

I wondered what her life was like in there with dead people coming and going like somber wind. When we played we always played outside. I didn't ask her if she wanted to come into my house and play because I was afraid she would ask me to come and play in her house.

Once I asked her if she was ever afraid of having dead people around the house.

'Why should I?' she said. 'They're dead. They can't hurt anybody.'

That was one way of looking at it, but it was not mine.

I also once asked if she ever listened to *Inner Sanctum*. I thought it would be very terrifying to listen to *Inner Sanctum* in a funeral parlor. It would be one of the worst experiences a person could ever have because listening to *Inner Sanctum* was scary enough but inside a funeral parlor! How could you stop from screaming or ever get to sleep again.

'Sure,' she said. 'But my favorite program is *Grand Central Station*. I like the sound of the trains and the people coming and going. They have interesting stories.'

'What about *Inner Sanctum*?' I said, returning to the subject of *Inner Sanctum* which was the most important thing on my mind. At a time like this who wanted to hear about *Grand Central Station*?

'*Inner Sanctum* is . . .' she said, pausing, ' . . . corny.'

CORNY! *INNER SANCTUM*. CORNY!

I was stunned.

'Corny,' she repeated, almost whispering it to get a certain dramatic effect.

If *Inner Sanctum* was corny, then how in the hell did she get such cold hands. Where did they come from? A Cracker Jack box? So when I played with her, I always avoided games that required hand holding.

She had long blond hair, but her hair wasn't cold, only her hands were cold and I treated them like the plague. Once she wanted to play ring-around-the-rosy, just the two of us, holding hands. I told her my mother was sick and I had to go get her a glass of water.

'I didn't know your mother was sick,' she said. 'You didn't mention it until now. How come?' The undertaker's daughter was too smart for her own good.

I was hard pressed for a reply.

If my mother had really been sick, that's the kind of

thing kids tell each other right off the bat. A sick mother is a newsworthy topic. I kept thinking as hard as I could. Meanwhile, avoiding her cold hands by putting my hands safely in my pockets and taking a couple of steps backwards toward my house.

But I couldn't think of a God-damn thing to say.

I just stood there like an idiot with an imaginary sick mother who didn't need tending to.

'I've got to get her a glass of water,' I finally said, desperately and ran into the house.

Someday I would be six years old, too, and be able to come up with fast questions, too.

'What are you doing in here?' my mother said when I came into the house. 'It's a beautiful day. Go outside and play.'

'I have to go to the toilet,' I said.

'Oh,' she said, rapidly losing her interest in me. 'Well, go to the toilet and then go back outside and play. I don't want to see you in here. It's too nice a day.'

I had no plans to stay inside. It was only a last ditch stand to keep away from the hands of the undertaker's daughter. I started toward a meaningless and unneeded pee-pee when there was a knock at the door.

My mother went to answer it.

Though I hadn't the slightest idea who was there, I knew that somehow it did not bring good tidings.

My mother opened the door.

I was sort of half-hidden on my way back to the toilet, watching my mother answer the door. Perhaps, I only thought I was hidden. I may have just been standing there without any attempt at camouflage.

It was the undertaker's wife.

She was surprised to see my mother standing there, looking so healthy.

'My daughter told me that you were sick,' she said. 'And I came over to ask if I could help out any.'

'That's nice of you,' my mother said. 'But I'm not sick.' I knew that my mother looked puzzled, though I could not see her face.

The undertaker's wife was looking directly at me, standing somewhere behind my mother, trying to be hidden. The expression on her face did not make me feel comfortable.

'My daughter told me that your son told her that you were sick, so I came right over. Obviously, you're not sick. I'm sorry to disturb you.'

The undertaker's wife took a couple of steps backwards.

'I appreciate your coming over, but I'm not sick. Would you like some coffee?' my mother said.

'Oh, no,' the undertaker's wife said. 'I've got something on the stove.'

Though suddenly I felt like a sinking ship, I still had enough curiousity to wonder what the undertaker's wife was cooking in the funeral parlor.

I had never really thought about them eating in there before, but of course they had to eat, and to eat you need to cook and she cooked breakfast, lunch and dinner in a place where dead people were briefly stored before something permanent was worked out for them.

I wondered how bacon and eggs tasted in a funeral parlor. I wondered how difficult it would be to eat ice cream in there. I didn't think there would be a big problem with it melting, even if it were a hot day.

'Well, I'm sorry that you came over for nothing,' my mother said. 'I'll have to get to the bottom of this.'

She did.

I was already there waiting for her.

All she had to do was turn around.

The next morning for my funeral-viewing pleasure, they held the funeral for a dead child. I was up bright and early and standing on my chair.

The funeral unfolded like the petals of a flower whose ultimate blossom was a small coffin coming out the door of the funeral parlor and on its way to the hearse and that final place where the hearse would take it and come back empty and the child wouldn't need its toys any more.

I of course had no idea that it was the funeral for a child until they brought the little coffin out; except for that one occasion I never knew who was being buried. I had no way of knowing if it was a man or a woman or a young person or an old person or just a person inbetween who had gotten unlucky.

The coffins were always closed and I did not know the specific nature of their contents. All I knew was that somebody dead was inside.

So I was stunned when the little coffin came out. It only needed two pallbearers. They carried the coffin as if it were a feather of death. I suddenly felt very uncomfortable because the coffin was my size. I didn't know if there was a dead little girl or a dead little boy inside. I know that this may sound horrible, but I half-wished that there was a dead little girl inside because a dead little boy was too close to home for me.

When the full impact of the child's funeral had modified itself into an unwholesome curiosity and interest in detail, I looked around for child mourners that were my age and the size of the coffin. There were none. There was not a single child.

That seemed very strange to me. Didn't the kid have any friends? God, what a poor kid, I thought, not a single friend. I could imagine the kid with no one to play with. I shuddered twice: once because the kid was dead and a second time because the kid was friendless.

There were about thirty people out there watching the small flower-bedecked coffin on its brief journey to the hearse which took care of the child ever having the possibility of a friend.

I was suddenly very sad because the child had never gotten to play hide-and-go-seek or kick-the-can or statues. The child had only played games that you play by yourself like playing with its dolls or the little boxed games that have animal heads you hold in your hands with two empty holes where the eyes should be and you roll two little silver balls around and around until you think you're going to go crazy before you give the animal some eyes or perhaps the child went on solitary tricycle rides past other children playing together who would have nothing to do with this dead kid.

I didn't know what fate was back, then, but if I had known I would not have wanted that kid's fate, not for all the tea in China, which was something people said all the time in 1940, but you don't hear it very much in 1979.

If you were to say, 'Not for all the tea in China,' right now, it would attract a lifted eyebrow, but back then it meant something. You were communicating.

I was really disturbed by the total lack of child mourners. I made a vow that I would be nicer to people, especially kids. I would start off that very day dedicating my energy to the gathering of many new friends and the instant renewal and replenishing of old friendships.

Under no conditions did I want to end up like that poor hapless child with nobody but adults at its funeral. Today I would be as friendly as I could with the undertaker's daughter.

I would even . . . I would even touch her hands. The worst thing in the world would be if I were to die and she wouldn't come to my funeral. That would be the final blow. Too bad it wasn't winter, so I could wear mittens. No, I shouldn't think like that. I promised myself that I would somehow hold her hands, so that she would come to my funeral.

They put the little coffin in the back of the hearse and placed around it wreaths and bouquets of flowers that seemed to swallow it whole. If you were alive and playing hide-and-go-seek, the back of that hearse would be a good place to hide. No one could find you in all those flowers.

WHERE WAS THE UNDERTAKER'S DAUGHTER? suddenly hit my mind like the first whack of a spanking. She wasn't at the funeral, but then I thought she obviously hadn't been a friend of the dead kid or she would be out there in a tiny black dress, dabbing a moon-white handkerchief to her eyes.

After the hearse had driven off and all the mourners had followed in its shadow like the morbid tail of a black kite, I thought some more about the undertaker's daughter and the child just on its way now to the cemetery where it would stay after everybody else came back. I didn't know the full dimensions of forever, but I knew that it was longer than waiting for Christmas to come.

I knew that forever was longer than 39 shopping days until Christmas.

Yesterday when I was playing with the undertaker's daughter and eventually fled the touching of her hands, that dead child must have already been in the funeral parlor getting ready for today. While we were playing outside, they could have been taking the blood out of that child and replacing it with embalming fluid.

I wondered if the undertaker's daughter had seen the dead child when it came in, and if the dead child had been a girl, she'd thought: *Well, here's somebody I'll never play dolls with* or she already knew that the child had no friends and so she didn't think about playing with her at all.

That's an awful thought, isn't it? but that's what I thought about while still standing on my chair perch staring at the sudden emptiness that had once been the funeral of a child.

I wondered why the undertaker's daughter wasn't afraid of dead people and then I thought somebody who prefers *Grand Central Station* to *Inner Sanctum* was capable of anything.

When I heard somebody stirring in the house a little later on, I got off my chair and pulled the window shade down. I put the chair back where it belonged. I didn't want anybody today criticizing my interest in funerals.

I was going back to bed and think all over again what I had seen today, but when I thought about that dead child lying in a coffin hidden by flowers and on its way to the cemetery, going back to bed did not seem like a good idea at all. I decided to spend as much time as possible the rest of the day standing on my feet, just to keep in practice.

A few months later, we moved and I never saw the undertaker's daughter again. She probably grew up, went to college and got married, then kids, etc. Maybe her hands even got warm.

I should probably think about her more often than I do. Actually, this is one of the few times that I have thought about her in years, maybe even longer.

The whole time that I lived beside the funeral parlor and watched the funerals like garden parties where I was always the uninvited guest seems to me now like a dream.

The undertaker's daughter has become a character in that dream. Did I really stand on a chair in my pajamas and watch funerals for pleasure? Did we really live in an apartment that had once been an active part of a mortuary? Did I dream the undertaker's daughter and her hands which were like white daisies growing on top of Mount Everest? Did I really hide from them until one day I saw the funeral of a dead child who had no friends and, not wanting to end up that way, courted her hands as if they had the desirability of warm mittens on a freezing winter day?

Yes, and I remember:

So the Wind Won't Blow It All Away
Dust . . . American . . . Dust

Finished with the undertaker's daughter and still carrying my sack of beer bottles, I'm halfway to the pond now where the people will arrive soon and start taking their furniture off the truck and setting up their highly original house beside the pond.

Childhood thoughts of early death continue to unravel in my mind, perhaps unpeel is a better and more accurate way of looking at it, like peeling an onion into a smaller and smaller circle with tears growing in my eyes until the onion is no more, all peeled away and I stop crying.

About five years after I left the dream-like address of an apartment beside a funeral parlor, I was living someplace else. World War II wasn't quite over. It was hanging on by the skin of its teeth, but you could feel that the end was very near.

For all practical purposes the War was over except that people were still getting killed every day and they would continue to get killed every day until the War was actually over.

The days were running out for the Japanese Empire as the days of my childhood were running out, and every step I took was a step that brought me nearer to that February 17th, 1948, orchard where my childhood would fall apart just like some old Roman ruins of a childhood, so we just sat around: the Japanese Empire and my childhood listening to each other breathing away the end.

The new place where I was living was two addresses away from, and approaching, the pond. The next address would take me a hundred miles to live in a dingy yellow apartment where the most important and expensive tube in the radio burnt out and we were too poor to afford another one, so at night our little Welfare family just sat around and looked at one another until it was time to go to bed.

There are no words to describe how important a radio was in those days.

The next address after the radioless apartment would be the auto court and out the front door of the cabin on the way to my beloved pond and its fishing furniture.

Meanwhile: Let's go back the two addresses and I'll tell a story of dead toys and silence. The new someplace I was living looked like an old house that rented for twenty-five dollars a month. Thank you, Welfare! We lived there long enough for the seasons to come and go once.

There were walnut trees in the front yard. There were apple and cherry trees in the back yard, which also contained a large building that was part garage, storage place and woodshed.

We didn't need the garage because we were too poor to own a car, but we were rich enough to use the woodshed. My mother cooked on a wood stove and we used wood to heat the house.

I always hated to chop wood.

The place also had a lot of lawn that needed to be mowed and I always hated to do that, too. In the spring we put in a garden, which I worked at with great hesitation. I was inbetween stepfathers at the time, so my mother did most of the work in the garden.

Let's face it: I was a kid who didn't like to do his chores. I tried to keep as much space between me and work as I could. I don't think I was lazy because I did a lot of other things, but they were always the things that I wanted to do, and I tried not to compromise my values.

I always liked old people, so I spent as much time with them as I could. They fascinated me like spiders, which I had a great deal of affection toward also. I could spend an hour with a spider web and be quite contented, but show me some weeds that needed pulling from the garden and I would exit a long large sigh like a billboard of desperation.

Late in the spring of 1945, a new kid moved into the house next door to 'ours.' He was older than me and really a good kid. He was the kind of kid other kids looked up to and wanted to be friends with.

I think he was twelve and he was a boy scout and shortly after moving in next door, he got a paper route because he had a bicycle and was ambitious. He was preparing himself for a positive life of accomplishment.

The bicycle looked brand-new even though it was prewar because he took such good care of it. I was not to have a bicycle until a couple of years later and my bicycle always looked shitty because I didn't care about its appearance. My bicycle started off by being blue but afterwhile it was so dirty that you couldn't tell what color it was and most people probably didn't care to begin with. The color of a kid's bicycle would not rank very high if you were to make a list of things people are interested in.

The boy next door always kept his clothes neat. With my clothes, half-the-time you didn't know if I was putting them on or taking them off. They were somewhere in the middle of coming and going simultaneously.

His parents really loved him.

I could tell by the way they talked to him.

My mother just barely tolerated my existence. She could take me or leave me. Once in a while she would go through short periods of intense affection toward me. It would always make me quite nervous and I was glad when she went back to just tolerating my existence.

You must pardon this cartoon-like Oedipus interlude because my relationship with my mother is not the point of this story.

The boy, being older than I, created the relationship between us. Older kids define the role younger kids act in their friendships.

He became a sort of abstract older brother to me. He was

always kind and understanding to me, but he created the distance between us. I would like to have seen him a couple of times a day, but we saw each other three or four times a week. This was his choosing. He controlled the amount of time we shared.

I didn't feel bad about it except that sometimes I wished I were older. Maybe that would have made a difference, probably not. Our interests were not that similar. He was interested in hard work and the satisfaction and products gained from it.

I liked to look at spider webs and listen to old people talk about the days when Teddy Roosevelt was President and watching members of the Grand Army of the Republic marching down the street in ever decreasing numbers toward the Twentieth Century.

You don't get the same material success from listening to old people talk as you do from having a paper route. I was always a good listener.

The boy kept his bicycle on the front porch if there was any chance of it raining but if the weather was good, he parked it under the long, drooping branches of a Queen Anne cherry tree.

The day the boy was killed in an automobile accident, the bicycle was parked under the cherry tree. It rained that same night. If he'd still been alive, he would have taken the bicycle and put it on the front porch. His parents were in the accident but they had not even suffered a scratch.

They came home by themselves just about twilight.

They were driving the same car the boy had been killed in that afternoon. It had been hardly damaged at all in the accident. The chances of anyone being killed in that accident were easily 1 in a 1,000,000. It was the type of accident that it's even rare to get injured in.

The boy was dead.

His parents got out of the car.

The entire neighborhood was watching them. Everybody knew what had happened because it was on the radio.

Some people looked out furtively from behind curtains and others just walked out on the front porch and stood there gawking.

I was in the branches of an apple tree when they drove up. I was about twenty feet above the ground. I had climbed the tree because I didn't know what else to do. I was sitting up there thinking about the boy being dead. Earlier I had gone into the woodshed and cried for a long time. I sat on the chopping block and cried my eyes out.

I wasn't crying any more when they drove up and got out of their car. Accidentally concealed, I was very close to them and I knew that they couldn't see me. I was in a deep green section of the tree that was like a room and a window formed in the leaves and I looked through the window at them getting out of the car.

She got out first.

Then he got out.

She closed her door but he didn't close his.

He stood there beside the open door of the car, not moving.

They just stood on opposite sides of the car, staring at their house. They didn't say anything and then he slowly closed his car door and they went into the house.

They turned on one light in the front room. They left the rest of the house dark. One of our neighbors, a very kindly woman, left her house across the street and came over and knocked on their front door.

They were very slow to answer.

'Can I help?' the woman said.

'No,' the boy's mother said.

'I don't know what to say,' the woman said.

'I know,' the boy's mother said.

'If you need any help. I'm right across the street,' the woman said.

'Thank you,' the boy's mother said. 'I think we'll just get some sleep. We're tired.'

Everybody in the neighborhood had been watching this. Nobody else came over that night. A few moments later the one light in the house went out.

I climbed very slowly down from the apple tree.

It rained that night.

The bicycle got wet.

The next morning the boy's father took the wet bicycle from underneath the long fruit-lush branches of the Queen Anne cherry tree and put it in the house.

They moved at the end of the month.

The neighbors watched silently. Nobody came over to say good-bye, not even the woman who had visited them the night their son had been killed. I looked over at her house but she wasn't watching. She was nowhere in sight.

When they moved, they didn't have the bicycle. It was not loaded on the moving van. I guess they must have gotten rid of it when I wasn't looking.

The house was dark and vacant for what seemed like an eternity, but it was only a week. The new tenants were very cheerful and friendly. They were too cheerful and friendly.

They held weekend beer parties and the driveway and the parking in front of their house overflowed with cars like a waterfall of pre-World War II metal.

The cars had the uneasiness of a dirty joke that is not funny, but perhaps it was only my imagination. Why shouldn't people have a good time? The War was almost over. We were tired of it. Sometimes I would climb up in the apple tree and quietly weep:

So the Wind Won't Blow It All Away
Dust . . . American . . . Dust

The last stop on the way to the pond was that yellow dingy Welfare apartment where the most expensive tube in the radio burnt out, leaving us with silent nights far distant from Christmas carols.

The apartment also had a gas stove in the kitchen.

We were all terrified of gas, especially my mother. She had a mind like a gray library filled with gas-leak death stories.

It was a stove that you had to light with a match and we were scared to death of it. Every meal was a nightmare with my mother having to build up her courage to cook. We usually had dinner around six, but with that gas stove, dinner arrived on the table as late as midnight.

Every meal was an exhausting experience that left us all completely drained right down to the bone where our marrow turned to dust caught in the vise of gas.

The worst it ever got was when my mother couldn't emotionally handle cooking any more and for one week, we had cornflakes for breakfast and the rest of the time we ate sandwiches.

We of course had no money and this was where Welfare had stashed us away. We lived there for three months and the radio was broken the entire time, so we just sat around in silence, waiting for the gas to get us.

My mother would wake up three or four times every night and check the stove for gas leaks. I was going to school at the time and I would ask the other kids what was happening on the radio.

They could hardly believe that I was not listening to the radio every night. It was inconceivable to them that somebody didn't have a radio.

Sometimes in the evening I would sit in front of our broken radio and pretend that I was listening to my favorite programs. My mother would pretend to read the *Reader's Digest*, but I knew that she really wasn't reading the magazine. She was just sitting there, listening for a gas leak.

The walls of the apartment were like dingy yellow roses and that's perhaps another reason why I disliked that apartment so much. It reminded me of all the funeral flowers that I had seen five years ago or was it twenty years ago? before I was even born.

The War seemed to have gone on forever, so that's why 1940 seemed such an incredible distance away, but when I stared at those walls long enough 1940 came closer and closer, and I could see the funerals moving in slow motion like old people waltzing in a movie.

I had very few friends because I was so exhausted all the time from the fear of dying by gas that it was very difficult for me to concentrate on anything or have the interest in trying to make friends.

So for that period of time, I just looked at other kids after I asked them what was on the radio. That was about the best I could do. Once I was awakened by the sound of my mother crying. I got out of bed. The apartment was dark except for a light shining under the bathroom door. She was in there crying. When she wasn't crying, she was just sitting in there repeating over and over again: 'Gas, gas, gas, gas.'

Then she would start crying again.

I went back to bed and wondered if I should cry. I thought about it for a long time, and decided not to. My mother was crying enough for both of us.

While we were living in that apartment, a child died in the neighborhood. She was about eight years old and one of three sisters who lived half-a-block away in a large house that had a yard cluttered with an enormous amount of toys. There were enough toys in their yard for an armada of children.

I'll bet there were at least nine balls in that yard, along with a convoy of tricycles and scooters. There were about ten Christmas trees of broken toys or toys deeply in trouble and on their way to being broken. It was only a matter of time and time was running out for them.

I wondered how those girls avoided serious injury from falling over their toys and breaking their necks or cutting their heads off with broken toys.

But everything went along smoothly until one of the girls died. Strangely enough, she did not die from a toy-related injury. She died of pneumonia which was always an ominous and frightening disease to me. Whenever I heard the word pneumonia, my ears perked up. To me it sounded like an awful way to die. I didn't want my lungs to slowly fill up with water and then to die by myself, drowning by means of myself, not in a river or a lake but in me drowning. I always had a feeling that you died from pneumonia when somebody was out of the room. You'd cry for help, but they wouldn't be there and when they came back, you'd be gone: drowned!

Whenever I heard of someone dying of pneumonia, young or old, I was obviously agitated. If I ever got pneumonia, I wanted whoever was there to tie a very long string on my finger and fasten the other end of the string to their finger and when they left the room if I felt I was dying, I could pull on the string and they'd come back.

I wouldn't die alone if there was a long piece of string between us.

Anyway, she died of pneumonia and Thank God, it wasn't me. When I heard she had died of pneumonia, I *really* said my prayers that night. I promised to be so good that I would make a saint seem like a sack of coal.

The day after she was buried all the toys in the front yard of their house disappeared and were very slowly replaced with totally different toys, but for a while that front yard looked like a toyless desert. I wondered why this had happened and finally I heard the story.

Her living sisters were afraid of their own toys because they didn't know what toys had belonged to the dead girl and they didn't want to play with the toys of somebody who was dead. They had played so freely and intensely that they could not separate the toys of the living from the toys of the dead.

Nothing their parents said could change their minds, so it was decided to give all the toys away to the Salvation Army where they would be changed into Christmas presents for the unsuspecting.

All the sisters had blond hair that was yellow like the apartment we lived in. Whenever I see a blond woman, I almost always think of that long-ago apartment that always teetered on the edge of either poisoning or blowing us up.

I wonder why I don't talk about my own sisters.

I guess this story is not about them.

Once my mother had a date with a man who was an unemployed roofer. I stayed at home and waited out her date. I read the *Reader's Digest* that she pretended to read. It had nothing to do with my life. There wasn't a single thing in there that reminded me of my existence.

I guess some people lived like the *Reader's Digest*, but I hadn't met any and at that time it seemed doubtful that I ever would.

My mother's date turned out to be quite short.

She came home around ten, early.

I heard the unemployed roofer's truck pull up outside. Maybe it helped being a roofer if you were four feet eleven, but it hadn't helped him because he didn't have a job. I knew that something was wrong because my mother slammed the truck door.

'Aren't you asleep yet?' she said when she came angrily in.

I tried to get on her good side, so I told her that I had been reading the *Reader's Digest*. I don't know why I thought that would put me in her good graces.

I was a strange kid.

I guess you could safely add *very*.

My mother just looked at me when I told her I had been

reading the *Reader's Digest*. It had not worked. I decided that it was time to go to bed and went very quickly there.

A few moments later I could hear my mother in the front room, repeating over and over again, in a hissing whisper: '*Gas, gas, gas, gas.*'

Looking back at it now, here in the forty-fourth year of life, my mother was the only leak in that apartment.

The next morning I got out of bed and put my clothes on very quietly, like a mouse putting on a Kleenex, and went over to the house where the little girl used to live before she died of pneumonia.

There were no toys in the front yard.

This was a couple of days after all the toys had been removed and given away at the vehement request of her very living sisters.

I stared at their absence.

I stared at their silence:

So the Wind Won't Blow It All Away
Dust ... American ... Dust

The sun had reversed its boredom and now had grown interesting as it began its descent which would soon open the beginning doors of night and the wind had died down making the pond as still and quiet as sleeping glass.

I had just reached my fishing dock and put down the gunnysack of beer bottles when I heard their truck coming down the road on the other side of the pond.

Ah, now my evening would really begin.

I got my fishing pole and carried it in one hand, the gunnysack of beer bottles slung over my shoulder with the other hand, and started on around the pond, which was about ¾'s of a mile in circumference.

I think the origin of the pond had been to get dirt to build the overpass, so that the trains could run under it. Once this pond had been just another field but now it was an overpass and a place for me to fish and an open living room for furniture.

I walked around the pond in the opposite direction from the route I had taken to the sawmill night watchman's gold mine of beer bottles.

There was a finger of water that branched off the pond that I had to walk around. The finger was forty yards long and about twenty yards wide. The water wasn't very deep in the finger and it was a great place for bluegills to spawn. The fishing was very good there, but you had to have some courage to fish that watery index off the pond because a strange old man had built a shack there.

All the kids I knew were afraid to fish there because they were afraid of the old man. He had long white hair like General Custer in an old folks home, denied the dignity and ceremony of meeting a few thousand Indians at the Little Big Horn.

He also had a long white beard that had a yellowish streak down the center caused by a constant overflow of chewing tobacco cascading out of his mouth.

He was the type of old man who looked as if he ate little children, but I had absolutely no fear of him. I met him the first time I was taken to the pond by a brand-new friend who asked me if I wanted to go fishing. I noticed a shack on the little finger-like bay off the pond.

I saw a man standing in front of it.

He was in the distance a ways, so I couldn't figure him out.

He had built a very sturdy little dock on the bay and he had a small boat tied up to it. He walked over from the shack to the dock and stood there looking at the water for a few moments. He didn't look up.

'Who's that?' I asked.

'A crazy old man,' my new friend said. 'Don't go over there. He hates kids. He hates everybody. He's got a big knife. It's as big as a sword. It looks like it's got rust on it, but it's really dried blood from kids.

'The fishing is really good, but no one goes over there. If that old man caught you, I don't know what would happen to you,' he said.

'I'll be back in a minute,' I said.

That little statement got me quite a reputation for being very brave and also crazy. I didn't mind the reputation from either end you looked at it. The distinction made me a sort of cockeyed hero, but that was all to end in the orchard that coming February.

The old man was very surprised when I walked up to him in a very friendly and relaxed style and said, 'Hello.' He was so surprised that he answered like the flipside of a well-mannered coin: 'Hello.'

'How's fishing?' I said.

'Good,' he said. 'But I don't fish.'

I looked down into the water and it was filled with spawning bluegills. The bottom of the pond was a ballet choreographed by courting bluegills. There were hundreds of bluegills there. I had never seen so many fish before.

I was really excited.

'Do you live here?' I asked, knowing of course that he lived there, but also knowing that it was important for him to say so because it would make him feel more comfortable, at ease to establish his own territory thus to make me a young, non-threatening guest.

'Yes,' he said. 'I've been living here since the Depression.'

When he said: Since the Depression, I knew everything was going to be OK.

The old man had built a shack out of packing crates. It was maybe eight by six feet and had a stovepipe coming out the side. It was summer and the screen door was closed to keep the mosquitoes out. I couldn't see into the shack because the way the screen door filtered, obscured the fading light of almost sundown.

He had a small table beside the shack with a bench that was a part of it. The table was made out of packing-crate wood and scrap lumber.

Everything was very clean and neat around the shack.

He had a small patch of corn, maybe forty stalks, and he was growing some potatoes and some green peas. There were also about a dozen tomato plants that were covered with small delicious-looking tomatoes.

He had built a small washbasin that was just a bucket stuck through a hole cut into a shelf that was nailed to the shack. When he wanted to wash, he just took the bucket from the hole in the shelf and got some water from the pond.

The shack had a flat tarpaper roof.

I talked to the old man for a few moments.

I think he was impressed by the fact that I wasn't afraid of him. Also, old people just tended to like me. I had a quality that appealed to them. Maybe they liked me because I was interested in them and listened to what they had to say. It could have been that simple.

I asked the old man if I could come back and visit him sometime. He responded by walking over and picking a really beautiful tomato and giving it to me.

'Thank you,' I said, starting to take a bite out of the tomato.

'Wait, before you do that,' he said, walking over to the shack and opening the screen door. I got a brief glimpse at the interior of his dwelling. All of his furniture seemed to be variations on packing-crate themes.

He came back out of the shack with the largest pepper shaker I had ever seen. 'Tomatoes taste best with pepper on them,' he said, offering me the shaker.

'You're not afraid that it's poison, are you?' he said.

'No,' I said, putting some pepper on my tomato.

'You can come back anytime you want,' he replied.

I took a bite out of the tomato.

'What do you think of tomato with pepper on it?' he said.

I've been eating it that way ever since.

He went and got himself a tomato.

Pretty soon tomato juice was mixed in with tobacco juice in his beard, which began to look like a poorman's rainbow.

When I got back to where I had left my new friend, he was gone. He came over to the cabin at the auto court that evening to see if I was still alive. He was very surprised when I answered the door.

'Jesus Christ!' he said. 'You're still alive.'

Then he asked me if I had seen the sword covered with all the dried blood of thousands of pond-slaughtered kids whose bones were buried under his shack like millions of loose toothpicks.

'It's not a sword,' I said. 'It's a huge pepper shaker.'

The kid didn't understand that, but he was very impressed anyway with what I had done.

I returned to visit the old man many times after that and to take apart and put back together his life like a huge puzzle in my mind, examining very carefully each piece and the totality of their effect.

The old man had been in World War I and was gassed by the Germans. Needless to say, when he mentioned the word gas, I was instantly fascinated and then he told me that it wasn't automobile gas or cooking gas, but poison gas and the Germans were sons-of-bitches for doing that to him because now he had only one lung and he couldn't do very much with his life except live here by the pond until one day the sheriff would come and tell him to move on and he'd have to find another pond somewhere.

The old man lived off a small pension that he got from The Government because he'd lost a lung in World War I. Other than this fact I didn't know anything else about him. He never talked about his family or ever being married or current and long-ago friends. I didn't know where he was born or anything about him. In his little packing-crate shack there were no personal items that gave a single clue to his past.

The old man had only things that he could use: clothing, cooking utensils, dishes and silverware, jars for storing food and some tools. He didn't have anything else.

He didn't have any old letters or a catfish postcard exploiting the possibilities of photography. He had made all his own furniture except for his stove out of packing crates and scraps of odd lumber.

The inside of his shack was so simple and honest that it

was almost like a glorified kids playhouse. He was living the kind of hermit life kids dream about living. He was an ancient breathing statue of Huckleberry Finn.

The old man measured carefully every movement that he made. He didn't ever waste a single gesture. Maybe it was only having one lung that made him so premeditated. I don't think he even blinked without first thinking about whether or not it was necessary.

Sometimes for reasons that were completely unknown to me I wished that he had a calendar. I had a feeling that he didn't know what day, month or year it was. I thought that he should at least know what year it was.

What was wrong with that?

It wouldn't hurt him to know that it was 1947.

The two things that he took the most pleasure in and that were the only incongruity in the personal history that he acted out at the end of a tiny bay on a small obscure pond were his dock and his boat.

Perhaps once he had something to do with the sea.

But I would never find out because he never spoke of it.

The dock was a thing of beauty to behold. It was perfectly constructed like a harpsichord and polished like a silver plate. It was about nine feet long and a yard wide. The pilings were finely carved timbers. Each one of them looked as if it had taken a year to carve. There were six of them. That means he must have started work on them in 1941, or so it seemed to me when I looked at them.

The dock itself was three ten-inch planks that were about two inches thick. They were also hand-carved and then finely polished until a king could have eaten off them. It would have been interesting to watch a king eat directly off a dock.

I would imagine that each plank took perhaps two years' carving and polishing, so that's six more years and now the construction of the dock reaches back to 1935, when I was born.

Maybe he started it on the day I was born.

Once I asked him again how long he had lived beside the pond and he was very hard-pressed to give me an exact time. 'I guess it's been a long time. Since the Depression,' he said, finally and somehow confirming my idea that he had started the dock on the day I was born.

Then I asked him when he had started working on the dock.

After an equally long pause, he said, 'About the same time.'

Yup, that confirmed it!

Every time I saw the dock after that, I felt good and considered it an unknown birthday present from him to me, though I never mentioned this to him.

Now: I'll talk about the boat.

It was like a little brother to the dock. It was totally handmade from an elegant wood that was varnished to a beautiful sheen like finely diluted sunlight. It was a very small boat. Maybe 4½ feet long and was, as I said earlier, a kid brother to the dock.

Sometimes I felt as if the old man was too big for such a small boat, but that was only a theoretical curiosity because I never once saw him in the boat.

It was always tied carefully, meticulously up to the dock. So what he had created was a holograph of boating which was not intended to actually move. It was just something to look at that pleased him very much and pleased me also because I thought it was another unknown birthday present from him to me.

In the background of the dock and the boat was a packing crate shack and a small patch of corn, green peas and tomatoes.

This was his life and time on earth.

The only vice the old man had was chewing a lot of tobacco. It stained his long white beard like a delicate garden constructed of a million tiny imperceptible daffodils.

Often when I looked at calendars back then, I thought about him lost in the geography of time, but finally not caring. Little did I know that I would end up the same way very soon:

So the Wind Won't Blow It All Away
Dust . . . American . . . Dust

The old man saw me coming a few months later with my fishing pole and my sack of beer bottles. He was sitting on his little packing-crate picnic-table bench, eating supper. His dock and boat were at total rest, total peace a few feet away from him. If he had been listening to some quiet dinner music, it could not have been any more peaceful than his dock and boat.

It looked as if he were eating some variation on the stew theme.

'Hello, there,' he said, cheerfully. 'Come to catch some of my bluegills?' He did have the best fishing in the pond right there.

'No,' I said. 'I'm on my way to the other side.'

He looked across the metal dish he was eating from to the other side of the pond where the people were still coming down the road in their pickup filled with furniture. It would take them a while to get there because the road was very bad and they always drove extremely carefully because they didn't want to lose any of their furniture.

At one place in the road, there were some miniature Grand Canyon ruts and the people took about five minutes to get through them and every time their truck just barely made it, but they drove the ruts so carefully that not even a lamp fell off.

Those ruts would give me enough time to be at their fishing place when they arrived, so I could watch them take their furniture off the truck from the very beginning piece. The first thing they would take off would be the couch and I would be there watching them.

'They're coming,' the old man said around a bite of stew in his mouth. He did a good job of balancing the stew in his mouth, so that I could understand what he was saying.

'Yeah,' I said. 'They're coming.'

'They come every evening this year,' he said. 'They came only four times last year, and they never came before that. Last year was the first year.'

I was very surprised when the old man said last year.'

I wondered if he knew last year was 1946.

'When they came last year,' he continued. 'They didn't bring any furniture with them. Just themselves. That's not a good place for catfish where they set all that stuff up. I wonder why they do that?'

The old man looked away from their approach and took a spoonful of his stew, which starred a lot of potatoes, featured carrots and peas, and from where I was standing, it looked as if a hot dog sliced very thin had a minor role in his stew. Floating in the center of the stew was a big dollop of catsup.

He ate off the ledge of the catsup, working his way to the rim of the metal dish, so the catsup was slowly sinking into the stew like a strange red island in the middle of an equally strange sea.

After the bite, which dashed some stew down his beard like lava coming from a volcano, he returned to watching their approach.

He paused before he said the next thing.

'I've never seen people bring their furniture when they go fishing. I've seen people bring camp stools, but not all their furniture.'

When he said this, it was not a form of criticism. It was just a simple observation that led to another bite from the movie on his plate called *The Old Man and the Stew*.

'Maybe they like to be comfortable when they fish,' I said.

'I suppose so,' he said. 'Wouldn't make much sense to bring all that furniture with them fishing if they didn't enjoy it.'

Then he stewed up again. This time he took an extraordinarily large bite. The runoff poured into his beard like Krakatoa.

'Well, I got to be on my way,' I said, so that I could be waiting for them when they got there. I liked to watch them unload the furniture and set it up from the very beginning. To me it was like watching a fairy tale unfold in front of my very eyes.

You don't see stuff like that very often and I didn't want to miss any of it, not even a single lamp. They had three of them that they set up. They looked just like any other lamp you'd see in a real house except the people had converted them from electricity to kerosene. It must have been interesting watching them do that. I wonder where they got the idea in the first place.

That's something that you just don't think up out of the ordinary.

Most people, I should say all people except them, just used the regular kerosene lamps you could buy in the store, but that type of thing obviously wasn't for them.

I wonder which one of them mentioned it to the other one first and what the expression on their face was and the next thing they said. I tried to imagine those words, but I couldn't because I wouldn't know what to say.

Would you?

But whatever was said in reply was the correct answer, the right thing and agreed upon and done.

The old man and his stew turned like a page in my life and then they were gone with his final words echoing in my mind as I headed toward the place where I would be there before they arrived and started setting up their furniture.

'If they want to catch catfish,' the old man echoed. 'They should set up their living room about fifty yards down the pond, right next to that dead tree. That's the best place for catfish in this pond.'

'They do all right where they set up their furniture,' I answered.

'Well, they'd do better for catfish if they put their living room in front of that dead tree.'

What?

I can still hear those last words now a third of a century later, and they still sound just as strange now as they did back then.

'I'll tell them,' I promised the old man, but of course I didn't tell them. They liked that place best for their furniture and they caught their share of catfish, so who was I to rock the boat?

I also don't think they would have listened to me anyway, and I certainly didn't want to make them angry at me because frankly they were the most interesting thing happen- ing in my life.

They were better than any radio programs I heard or movies I saw that summer.

Sometimes I wished there was a set of them like toys that I could take home with me and play with: Carved wooden miniatures of the man and the woman and all their furniture and the truck (it was all right for that to be metal) and a green cloth that was shaped just like the pond with everything on it the way it actually was.

I also wished that I had miniatures of the old man and his shack and his garden and of course the dock and his boat.

What an interesting game that would be.

Sometimes I tried to think of a name for it just before I fell asleep but I never could think of a good name for it and afterwhile it got lost in my dreams because I couldn't keep up with it.

I arrived at the place where their living room would be set up at the pond's edge just about a minute or so before they got there.

While the minute passes before they get here with their furniture, there will be a huge INTERRUPTION like a black wet *Titanic* telegram or a telephone call that sounds like a man with a chain saw cutting up a cemetery at midnight or just the very rude distraction of death itself, the final end of all childhoods including mine which started to dramatically begin its descent when I passed the restaurant that February rainy afternoon in 1948 and should have gone inside and gotten a hamburger and a Coke. I was hungry, too. They would have been a welcome addition to my existence.

There was not a single reason in the world for me to walk past the restaurant and look in the window of the gun shop next door. But I did and the dice were getting ready to be thrown.

There was a beautiful-looking .22 caliber rifle in the window. I had a .22. Looking at that gun made me think about my gun, and when I thought about my gun, I thought about the fact that my gun didn't have any bullets. I had been planning on getting some for the last couple of weeks.

If I had some bullets, I could go out and shoot.

I could go to the junkyard and shoot bottles and cans and any abandoned old thing that looked attractive through my sights or there was an old apple orchard that had rotten apples still clinging to its leafless branches. It was fun to shoot rotten apples. They exploded when a bullet hit them. It was the kind of effect that kids love if they're slightly bloodthirsty for one reason or another and can dump their aggressions on passed-away objects like rotten apples.

I had a friend who liked to shoot apples, too, but he didn't like to go to the junkyard to practice the little decisions of destruction that a .22 rifle can provide a kid. But I couldn't shoot anything one way or another if I didn't have any bullets.

Some bullets . . . . or a burger, a burger . . . . or some bullets . . . . paddled back and forth in my brain like a Ping-Pong ball.

The door to the restaurant opened just then and a satisfied customer came out with a burger-pleased smile on his face. The open door also allowed a gust of burger perfume to escape right into my nose.

I took a step toward the restaurant but then I heard in my mind the sound of a .22 bullet turning a rotten apple into instant rotten apple juice. It was a lot more dramatic than eating a hamburger. The door to the restaurant closed escorting the smell of cooking hamburgers back inside like an usher.

What was I to do?

I was twelve years old and the decision was as big as the Grand Canyon. I should have gone to neutral territory to think it over instead of just standing right there in the battleground of their beckoning.

I could have gone across the street to a magazine store and looked at comic books while I though about how seriously I wanted a box of apple-splattering bullets or a delicious hamburger with lots of onions on it.

I could have thought about it while looking at comic books until the owner of the store started giving me the evil eye because obviously I was not a potential comic-book purchaser. I was just a kid hanging out with Superman and Batman while I made up my mind.

Too bad Superman couldn't have told me what to do.

SUPERMAN: Kid, go get a burger.

ME: Yes, sir!

SUPERMAN: And don't forget the onions.

ME: How did you know I liked onions?

SUPERMAN: If you're faster than a speeding bullet and more powerful than a locomotive and able to leap tall buildings with a single bound, onions aren't that hard.

ME: Yes, sir!

SUPERMAN *(flying away):* Be kind to your kitten! *(I would have to think that one over because I didn't have a kitten. Anyway, not one that I could remember. Maybe Superman knew something that I didn't know. Of course he did!)*

ME: I promise, Superman!

What did I have to lose?

Yeah, everything would have been different if Superman would have told me to get a hamburger. Instead I walked across the street to the gun shop and bought a box of .22 shells. The hamburger had lost. The sound of instant rotten apple sauce had won.

I have replayed that day over and over again in my mind like the editing of a movie where I am the producer, the director, the editor, scriptwriter, actors, music, and everything.

I have a gigantic motion picture studio in my mind where I have been working constantly on this movie since February 17th, 1948. I have been working on the same movie for 31 years. I believe that this is a record. I don't think I will ever finish it.

I have, more or less, about 3,983,421 hours of film.

But it's too late now.

Whereas I could never find a name for my pond game, I've always had a title for my movie starting with the day I bought the bullets instead of the hamburger. I call my picture *Hamburger Cemetery*.

After I bought the bullets, I didn't have any more money for a hamburger, so I started home. The box of bullets felt very good in my pocket. When I got home I would show them to my gun. I would load and unload my gun a couple of times. That would make the gun happy because guns like bullets. They are nothing without bullets. They need bullets like a camel needs the desert.

My gun had an interesting story about how it got into my life. I knew this boy whose parents didn't like him because he was always getting into trouble. He was fourteen, smoked, had a reputation as a well-known masturbator and had been picked up by the police half-a-dozen times though he had never been formally charged with anything. His parents always got him off.

His father had some thread-thin political influence that was left over from having had a bright future in local politics about ten years ago. He had lost his political future when he was arrested the second time for drunk driving and running over an old lady who broke like a box of toothpicks being stepped on by an elephant. She was in the hospital so long that when she got out, she thought it was the Twenty-First Century.

But he still had a few political debts owed him – before he ran over the old lady there was talk in high places about him being the next mayor – and he collected them whenever he went and got his son out of jail.

Anyway, the boy's parents didn't like him and after the last time he was arrested they decided not to let him sleep in the house any more. From now on after that, he was to sleep out in the garage. He could take his meals in the house and bathe and go to the toilet there, but those were the only times they wanted him in there.

To make sure that he got the point of their dislike, they did not provide him with a bed when they exiled him to the garage. That's where I come in and the gun comes in.

The boy had a .22 caliber pump rifle. I had for some unknown reason, I can't remember why, a mattress.

Just after his parents Siberia-ized him to the garage, he came over to visit me. I'll never totally know why because we were not that good of friends. In the first place, his reputation as a prodigious masturbator did not weigh well with me. I had jacked off a few times you know, but I was not interested in making it a career.

Also, he had eyes that were born to look at things that he could steal. I of course stole a few things, but I wasn't interested in stealing everything. And, finally, I didn't like his smoking all the time and trying to get me to smoke. I just wasn't interested in smoking but he kept insisting that I smoke with him.

Though he was fourteen and I was twelve and he was bigger than me, for some strange reason he was almost afraid of me. I encouraged his fear by telling him a few gory lies about my prowess in hand-to-hand combat with other twelve-year-old kids. I also told him that I had once beaten up a seventeen-year-old. That really registered with him.

'It doesn't matter how big they are. You hit them in the right place and they all fall. You just have to know that place,' I said, finishing up my tale of Jack Dempsey-like heroics that convinced him into being a minor coward around me, which I enjoyed enormously but not enough to have him for a friend to bully.

As I said earlier, he just had too many things going that were not in his favor.

And then he arrived one day and told me his story of parental rejection and how he had to sleep in the garage and he didn't have anything to sleep on.

The cement floor was cold.

'I don't know what I'm going to do,' he said.

I knew what he was going to do. The words had barely escaped his mouth when I had it all planned out. What was to form an eternal breach between him and his parents and eventually lead him to doing three years in the pen for stealing a car and then a marriage with a spiteful woman ten years older than him who had five children who all grew to hate him, causing him to gain his only and ultimate solace in this world by buying a telescope and becoming an extremely incompetent but diligent astronomer, was to work to my brief advantage.

'Mommy, where's Daddy?'

'Looking at the stars.'

'Mommy, do you hate Daddy, too?'

'Yes, child. I hate him, too.'

'Mommy, I love you. Do you know why?'

'Why?'

'Because you hate Daddy. It's fun to hate Daddy, isn't it?'

'Yes, child.'

'Why does Daddy look at the stars all the time, Mommy?'

'Because he's an asshole.'

'Do assholes always look at the stars, Mommy?'

'Your father does.'

He had his telescope in the attic and he was always confusing his constellations. He could never get it quite straight between what was Orion and what was the Big Dipper. For some strange reason he couldn't accept that the Big Dipper looked like a big dipper, but at least he wasn't in jail for stealing cars.

He worked hard and gave his wife all his money and she went to bed with the postman every chance she got. It was barely a life but being always confused about the Big Dipper gave it a fingernail-clipping continuity and meaning. 'How could it be the Big Dipper if it looks like a big dipper?' was the way he approached it.

But all that was years in the future and now he was standing in front of me bedless and telling me all the details.

Changing the subject completely, I put my plan in effect by asking him if he still had that old .22 rifle of his.

'Yes,' he said, looking slightly bewildered at the turn of mental events. 'What does that have to do with anything? What am I going to do? I'll catch pneumonia out there in the garage.'

I successfully concealed my instantaneous revulsion when he said the dreaded word pneumonia. I had more serious things on my mind than to be rattled by the idea of pneumonia.

'No, you won't,' I said.

'How do you know?' he said.

'I've got a mattress,' I said.

He looked at me.

'I've got a mattress, too,' he said. 'But my folks won't let me take it out of the house into the garage.'

Good! I thought: My plan is a certain success.

'I've got an extra mattress,' I said, emphasizing the word EXTRA. He was impressed, but he knew that there was a catch to it. He waited.

I made it simple and sweet using the English language like a brain surgeon ordering a sequence of nerve events with his scalpel.

'I'll trade you my mattress for your .22.'

His face showed that he didn't like that idea. He took out a twisted and hunchbacked cigarette butt. It looked as if he had found it in the Hugo novel.

Before he could light it, I said, 'I just read someplace that it's going to be a . . . very . . . cold . . . winter.' I dragged the key words out until they sounded as long as December.

'Ah, shit,' he said.

That's how I got the gun that led me to making the fatal decision to get a box of bullets instead of a hamburger.

If his parents hadn't made him go live in the garage, I never would have traded my mattress for his gun. Even if they'd still made him go live in the garage, but had given him a mattress, I wouldn't have had that gun. I got the gun in October of 1947 when time-sequenced nature was beginning to close the pond down for winter.

When the first cold rainy winds of a big autumn storm blew across the pond, everything changed, but of course none of this has happened yet.

It is the future.

The present is watching their truckload of furniture drive/rattle down the road toward me, but somehow they never seem to get any closer.

They are like a mirage that refuses to have any responsibility toward reality. It just stands there satirizing actual things. I try to make it respond like reality but it refuses. It won't come any closer.

They and their truck are pasted like a child's drawing against the fourth dimension. I want them to come, but they won't come, so I am catapulted into the future where it is November 1948 and the February-17th apple orchard event is history. The court found me not guilty of criminal negligence in the shooting.

A lot of people wanted me sent to reform school, but I was found innocent. The subsequent scandal forced us to move and now I'm living in another town where nobody knows what happened in that orchard.

I am going to school.

I'm in the seventh grade and we are studying the American Revolution, but I have no interest in the American Revolution. I am only interested in everything that I can find out about hamburgers.

Somehow I believe that only a complete knowledge of hamburgers can save my soul. If I had gotten a hamburger that February day instead of bullets, everything would have been different, so I *must* find out all that I can about hamburgers.

I go to the public library and pour over books like intellectual catsup to gain information about the hamburger.

My desire for hamburger knowledge dramatically increases the level of my reading. One of my teachers gets alarmed. She calls in my mother trying to find out the origins of my gigantic intellectual leap.

My mother can only help by saying that I like to read a lot.

This does not satisfy the teacher.

One day the teacher asks me to stay after school. The teacher is becoming obsessed by my newly-found reading level.

'You're reading a lot,' the teacher says. 'Why?'

'I like to read,' I say.

'That's not good enough,' the teacher says, her eyes brightening. I'm beginning not to like this at all.

'I talked to your mother. That's what she also told me,' the teacher says. 'But you don't think I believe that, do you?'

I'd had teachers before who were strict disciplinarians and wouldn't think twice about whacking a kid, but this teacher was rapidly becoming dangerous right in front of my eyes.

'What have I done wrong?' I say. 'I just like to read.'

'That's what you think!' the teacher yells, loud enough to summon the principal who takes her away to his office, sobbing hysterically.

Following a period of recuperation, a month's sick leave, total rest, the teacher was transferred to another school. After a series of substitute teachers, we got a new permanent teacher who didn't give a damn about my reading, so I continued gaining the reading tools to aid in my exploration of the hamburger and possible redemption through a complete knowledge of its origins, quirks and basic functioning.

Looking back on it now, I guess I used the hamburger as a form of mental therapy to keep from going mad because what happened in that orchard was not the kind of thing that causes a child to have a positive outlook on life. It was the kind of thing that challenged your mettle and I used the hamburger as my first line of defense.

Because I looked older than I actually was – I was thirteen, then, but I was tall for my age, so that I could easily be mistaken for fifteen – I passed myself of as a high school student who was a reporter for the school paper and doing an article on hamburgers.

This gave me access to almost all the fry cooks in the new town where we had been forced to move. Ostensibly, I interviewed them about their experiences cooking, but always worked the interview around to their involvement with hamburgers. The interview would start out being about one thing and would always end up being about hamburgers.

A bright young high school reporter (me): When was the first time that you cooked a hamburger?

A Mexican fry cook approaching forty the hard way: Do you mean professionally?

Reporter: Yes, professionally or just as an amateur.

Mexican Fry Cook: Let me think. I was just a kid when I cooked my first hamburger.

Reporter: Where was that?

Mexican Fry Cook: Albuquerque.

Reporter: How old were you?

Mexican Fry Cook: Ten.

Reporter: Did you enjoy cooking it?

Mexican Fry Cook: What was that question again?

Reporter: Was it fun cooking your first hamburger?

Mexican Fry Cook: What kind of article did you say this was?

Reporter: It's about cooks here in town.

Mexican Fry Cook: You sure ask a lot of questions about hamburgers.

Reporter: You cook a lot of hamburgers, don't you?

Mexican Fry Cook: But I cook a lot of other things, too. Why don't you ask me about grilled cheese sandwiches?

Reporter: Let's finish up with hamburgers. Then we'll move onto other things: grilled cheese sandwiches, chili.

Mexican Fry Cook: I've never been interviewed before. I'd love to talk about chili.

Reporter: Don't worry. We'll talk about it. I'm very certain my readers want to hear everything you know about chili, but first let's finish up with hamburgers. That hamburger you cooked when you were ten years old was an amateur hamburger, wasn't it?

Mexican Fry Cook: I guess so. No one paid me to cook it.

Reporter: When did you cook your first professional burger?

Mexican Fry Cook: Do you mean when I got paid to cook my first hamburger?

Reporter: Yes.

Mexican Fry Cook: That would have been my first job. 1927 in Denver. I went to Denver to work in my uncle's garage but I didn't like working on cars, so my cousin had a little cafe near the bus depot and I went down there and started helping him out cooking and pretty soon I had a shift all my own.

I was seventeen.

I've been cooking ever since, but I cook a lot of other things than hamburgers. I cook—

Reporter: Let's finish with the burgers first and then we'll get onto other things. Did you ever have any remarkable experiences cooking a hamburger?

Mexican Fry Cook (now beginning to show a little concern): How can you have a remarkable experience cooking a hamburger? I mean, you just put the patty on the grill and cook it. You turn it over once and put it on a bun. That's a hamburger. That's all there is to it. Nothing else can happen.

Reporter: What's the most hamburgers that you ever cooked in a day?

Mexican Fry Cook: I've counted a lot of things in my life but I've never counted hamburgers. People order them and I cook them. That's all I know about it. I mean, sometimes I'm busier than other times and sometimes when I'm busy people order a lot of hamburgers, but I've never counted them. I've never even thought about counting hamburgers. Why should I count hamburgers?

Reporter (undaunted): Who is the most famous person you ever cooked a hamburger for?

Mexican Fry Cook: What's the name of the paper you're writing for again?

Reporter: The Johnson Union High School Gazette. We have a large circulation. A lot of people out of high school read our paper instead of the *Johnson City Herald.*

Mexican Fry Cook: Do your readers want to know this much about hamburgers? I had some very interesting experiences in the War, cooking in the South Pacific. Once I was cooking breakfast on Kwajalein when a Japanese bomber—

Reporter (interrupting): That sounds very exciting but let's finish up with the hamburgers, so we can get onto other subjects. I know that talking about hamburgers may seem dull to you a professional, but my readers are fascinated by hamburgers. My editor told me to find out as much as I could about hamburgers. Our readers eat a lot of hamburgers. Some of them eat three or four hamburgers a day.

Mexican Fry Cook (impressed): That's a lot of hamburgers.

Reporter: In my article I'll mention the name of this restaurant and you'll be getting a lot more business. I wouldn't be surprised if this place became famous. Who knows. You might even become part owner because of this interview.

Mexican Fry Cook: Did you get the spelling of my name right?

Reporter: G-O-M-E-Z.

Mexican Fry Cook: That's right. What else do you want to know about hamburgers? What the hell! If people want to know about hamburgers, I sure as hell won't stand in the way.

Reporter: Have you ever felt sad cooking a hamburger?

Mexican Fry Cook: Only if I'd spent all my money on a girl or if a girl left me. Then I'd feel sad even if I was cooking pancakes. The most trouble I have in this world is with girls. I always get girlfriends who give me a lot of trouble. They take all my money and I feel bad afterwards, but some day I'll meet the right one, I hope. In the meantime, yeah, girls make me feel sad when I'm cooking and that includes hamburgers.

I'm dating a girl now who's a beauty operator. All she wants me to do is take her out to fancy restaurants and nightclubs. I have to work two shifts to keep her in restaurants and nightclubs, and you can bet your life that she won't eat here.

I once asked her if she wanted to eat dinner here. Of course I wasn't cooking. It wasn't my shift, but she said, 'Are you kidding?' Three hours later she ate so many shrimp at this fancy seafood place that I had to hock my watch the next day. She wouldn't eat here if this was the last place on earth.

I stood there with my notebook imitating as if I were taking down notes about his love life that he was really getting into now, but they weren't notes. They were just nonsense symbols and useless abbreviations in my notebook. They could not be used for anything, but whenever he mentioned hamburgers my notes became as bright and clear as a searchlight.

Reporter (interrupting the boring tragedy of his life. He really wasn't a very good-looking man. The only reason women would go out with him was that he worked sixteen hours a day cooking hamburgers and he would spend all his money on them): Did you ever feel happy cooking a hamburger?

Mexican Fry Cook: If it was the last hamburger of the day, and I was going out on a date afterwards, I might feel happy because I was getting off work and was going to maybe have some fun with a girl.

I ingeniously ended the interview by keeping him away from cooking breakfast on Kwajalein during the War and a Japanese bomber – Also, his chili ended up being very much left out in the cold. As I was leaving the cafe, he began to have second thoughts about the interview. 'When is this interview going to come out?' he said.

'Soon,' I said.

'Do you really think people want to know so much about hamburgers?' he said.

'It's the latest rage,' I said.

'I didn't know that,' he said.

'Keep those burgers coming,' I said. 'And you'll be a very famous person.'

'Famous for cooking hamburgers?'

'No one ever heard about Charles Lindbergh until he flew across the Atlantic, did they?'

'Yeah,' he said. 'But cooking hamburgers is a lot different.'

'Not that different,' I said. 'Think about it.'

'OK,' he said. 'I'll think about it, but I can't see what hamburgers have to do with Charles Lindbergh. I don't think they have anything in common.'

'Let me put it another way,' I said, rapidly approaching the door on my way out. 'Lindbergh took some sandwiches with him to eat when he flew across the Atlantic. Right?'

'I guess so,' he said. 'I think I remember something like that.'

'Well, none of them were hamburgers,' I said. 'They were all cheese sandwiches.'

'All cheese?' he said.

'Not one hamburger,' I said, nodding my head solemnly.

'Everything would have been completely different if he had taken three hamburgers with him.'

'How do you figure that?' the Mexican fry cook said. 'If he took hamburgers with him, they'd just get cold and a hot burger tastes a lot better than a cold burger.'

'If Charles Lindbergh had taken three cold hamburgers,' I said. 'With him when he crossed the Atlantic all by himself in *The Spirit of St Louis*, he would have been famous for the cold hamburgers and not the actual flight itself, right?'

Before he could reply to that I had closed the door to the cafe from the outside. I had a feeling that whatever girl he saw that night, no matter how many orders of shrimp she ate, she would make him feel better.

I interviewed about two dozen fry cooks in my quest for burger Satori. I went to meat markets and interviewed butchers about the quality of hamburger meat, personal feelings and reminiscences and anything odd they might tell me about the making of hamburger.

I went to bakeries where the hamburger buns were baked and interviewed bakers to find out everything I could about the baking of hamburger buns and any stories related to their baking.

An old baker who had heart trouble told me that he always prayed when he put the hamburger buns in the oven to bake. I asked him if he prayed when he took them out. He said no.

I wanted bizarre stories about hamburger buns!

I searched high and low for burger information.

I interviewed over fifty chosen-at-random victims to tell me their personal experiences eating burgers. I wanted unusual burger stories. I wanted happy burger yarns and amusing incidents concerning the burger.

I wanted tales of hamburger terror.

I collected a dozen file cards dealing with people who got sick eating hamburgers. A woman told me that she once got so sick eating a hamburger that she fell off the front porch.

There was no extreme that I wouldn't go to find out more about the hamburger.

I looked for hamburger references in the Bible. I was certain that there must be an overlooked reference to a burger in the Book of Revelations. Maybe the Four Horsemen of the Apocalypse liked hamburgers.

My days and nights were nothing but fields of burgers for months and months after we had to move away from the February-17th incident with the rifle in the apple orchard.

Well, the truck and its load of furniture are still pasted like some kind of greeting card to a mirage which is the past. I should let them advance and take their rightful places beside the pond.

They are only about a hundred yards away from the pond and all I have to do is let go of them and they will drive right up here where I am sitting.

But for some strange reason, I won't let the people drive up to the pond and take their furniture off the truck and go about their evening's fishing a third of a century ago.

I'm quite certain they are dead by now.

They were in their late thirties back then, and they were so huge and fat that they probably died of heart attacks maybe twenty years ago when they were in their early fifties.

They both had that early-fifties-heart-attack look to them.

First, one would die and then the other would die, and that would be the end of them, except for whatever I write down here, trying to tell a very difficult story that is probably getting more difficult because I am still searching for some meaning in it and perhaps even a partial answer to my own life, which as I grow closer and closer to death, the answer gets further and further away.

In my mind I can see two extra large graves in the middle of nowhere with not a single piece of fishing furniture in sight.

It's totally over for them now: no more truck, no more each other, no more couch right beside the edge of the pond with them sitting there fishing into the dark, illuminated by three electric lamps converted to kerosene and a fire coming from a small wood stove with no pipe because you don't need a pipe when there's no roof or house or room, just the outdoors beside a pond in perfect harmony with their fantasy.

I'm going to leave them in the past, driving against reality for a little while longer. They don't know how slowly they are travelling to the pond because they've been dead for so many years now.

They will remain for a while longer two American eccentrics freeze-framed in grainy black and white thirty-two years ago at sunset:

So the Wind Won't Blow It All Away
Dust ... American ... Dust

David didn't like to shoot at the junkyard. He said it was boring. He was two years older than I and my secret friend. I was a sort of social outcast in school because of my obvious poverty and ways that were sometimes hard for other classmates to understand. Basically, my only claim to fame was my lack of fear of the old man who lived at the pond.

That kind of fame has its limitations.

You're not going to be voted the most popular kid in your class because you're not afraid of an old man who has only one lung and lives in a packing-crate shack beside a pond that doesn't even have a name.

But I was smart and a year ahead in school and attending junior high.

David and I did a lot of things together but we always did them alone. I was not admitted into his social group. I wasn't invited to any parties that he gave or to drop by his house. We always met on the sly.

David was an enormously popular kid: the most outstanding athlete in school and class president. Whenever anything was voted on, he got it. His grades were straight A's.

He was tall and slender and had fine blond hair and all the girls were madly in love with him. His parents worshipped the ground he walked on. Whereas a lot of other kids got into some kind of trouble, he always got into achievement and glory. He had everything going for him. His future was unlimited.

I played a hidden role in his life.

He liked the odd paths of my imagination.

He could talk to me about things that he couldn't talk to other kids about. He told me that he wasn't as confident and self-assured as everybody else thought he was, and that sometimes he was afraid of something that he couldn't put his finger on.

'I'm scared of something, but I don't know what it is,' he once said. 'It bothers me all the time. Sometimes I get very close to knowing what it is, but then when I can almost see it, it fades away and I'm left alone, wondering what it is.'

He was also the best dancer in school and sang 'Blue Moon' at student body assemblies. His version of 'Blue Moon' made the girls' hearts beat like the hearts of excited kittens.

David went out with a girl who was a cheerleader and president of the drama club and played the leading role in all their plays. By any standard, she was the prettiest girl in school.

I admired her from a distance, but I had a strong feeling that she had no idea we shared space on the same planet. Their going out together was the biggest single topic in school, but he never once mentioned her to me.

He and I would meet at odd times in a constant but almost accidental pattern. We saw each other two or three times a week but seldom were our meetings worked out in advance.

They just happened.

The day after I got the bullets when I should have gotten the hamburger, I bumped into him at the bicycle rack at school.

He was of course alone. He had been talking to another kid as I walked up, but he finished his conversation with him and he left just as I arrived.

So there we were alone together again.

'Hi,' he said. 'Let's go for a ride.'

His bicycle was in perfect condition. His spokes and chain shined like silverware. Mine were muddy and rusty. The paint on his bicycle looked brand-new. My paint just looked.

He led the way and somehow we were riding along a street where not many other kids lived or rode their bicycles. It was almost a kidless zone.

We didn't say anything as we rode along until he started

talking. I always let him initiate the conversation. He was the king of our friendship and I was his vassal. I didn't mind. I had other things to think about. Though he seemed to be the crystallization of excellence and normality, I found him almost as odd as I was.

Finally, he spoke: 'I had a dream about it last night,' he said.

'Could you see it?' I said.

'No, just before I can see it, the damn thing disappears and I wake up feeling strange and unhappy. I've had dreams about it all week,' he said. 'I wish I could see it just once. That's all I ask.'

'Maybe you'll see it someday,' I said.

'I hope so,' he said.

We bicycled by a cat.

The cat didn't pay any attention to us.

It was a huge gray cat with enormous green eyes. They were like very small ponds.

'I got some bullets for my gun,' I said. 'Do you want to go shooting tomorrow?'

'Not at the junkyard,' he said.

'No, the orchard,' I said. 'We'll shoot rotten apples.'

'That sounds like a good idea,' he said. 'I've been feeling so bad recently because of those dreams that I'd like to shoot some rotten apples.'

Then he smiled. 'Yeah, I'll shoot some rotten apples and then I'll feel better.'

'It beats doing nothing,' I said.

We pedalled another block and then we saw another cat. This one was smaller than the first one, but it was gray, too. Actually, it looked identical to the first cat except for its size and it also had enormous green pond-like eyes.

'Did you see that cat?' he said.

'Yeah,' I said. Then I knew what he was going to say next but I let him say it first.

'It looks like that other cat, but it's smaller,' he said.

Those were the exact words that I knew he was going to say.

'I wonder if they're related,' I said.

'Yeah, maybe so,' he said. 'The big cat's the mother and the small cat is the son or daughter.'

'Makes sense to me,' I said.

'For some strange reason those cats make me think about those people who brought their furniture to the pond last summer,' he said. 'Remember when you took me to see them?'

'Yeah,' I said.

'They were really strange people. I wonder why those cats made me think about them,' he said.

I wondered about that, too.

I put the two cats together in my mind and I couldn't figure out why they made him think about the pond people and their furniture. The cats' eyes reminded me of ponds but that was as far as I could travel with it.

'You got to know those people real well,' he said. 'Why did they bring their furniture with them?'

'I guess they just wanted to be comfortable while they fished,' I said.

'They came there every night, didn't they?' he said. 'What did they do with all the fish they caught? I mean, they were both huge people but nobody could eat that much fish. When I was there with you, they caught about thirty fish and they kept them all. Those people couldn't eat thirty fish night after night. That's fifteen fish apiece.'

What David was talking about was something that had never really crossed my mind before. What did they do with all those fish? because they always kept every fish they caught. They even kept the smallest ones. They put all the fish on a big stringer in the water and fastened it to the shore with a railroad spike. They always brought a special very heavy hammer with them to pound the spike in with.

It was a part of their ritual.

That means that every week they must have eaten at least 105 fish apiece and some of the fish were big catfish and sometimes they caught bass that weighed up to five pounds.

They always cooked dinner at the pond on a wood-burning kitchen stove, but of course they didn't need a pipe because there wasn't any ceiling to their kitchen.

As we pedalled along, I was thinking about how they ate everything for dinner but fish. They cooked a lot of hamburgers and pork chops, and liver and onions, and they cooked potatoes in various ways and sometimes she baked cornbread and every once in a while a pie, but she did not cook a single fish.

Every caught fish always went on the stringer and back into the pond where it was anchored to the shore with a railroad spike.

What did they do with all those fish?

Did they eat them for breakfast?

That would be fifteen fish apiece every morning for breakfast or if they ate them at lunch it would be the same amount of fish, even if they divided the fish between breakfast and lunch that would still be seven or eight fish apiece for each meal. That's a hell-of-a-lot of fish and I don't think people can eat that much fish.

Maybe they gave the fish to their friends. I had to rule that out because these people didn't look as if they ever had any friends. Wait, that's not correct. I remember them once mentioning some friends they knew a long time ago, but you can't give fresh fish to people that you haven't seen in years.

If they gave the fish to their cat, it would have to be a lion. They didn't look like cat lovers either.

Out of the clear blue or I should say just-starting-to-rain February late twilight, David had opened a new mystery to me and a different viewpoint of the pond people.

What in the hell did they do with all those fish? It was too late now to find out because it was winter and bad weather had closed the pond down in October.

It was a mystery, then, and would always remain a mystery forever because I never saw them again.

Growing bored with too many fish for too few people, David changed the subject. 'When did you say you wanted to go shooting rotten apples in that old orchard?'

Today was Friday.

Tomorrow would be Saturday: no school.

'How about tomorrow?' I said.

'Fine, maybe it will make me forget about that thing in my dreams,' David said. 'I sure wish I knew what it looked like. I can almost see it but not quite.'

'Shooting some apples will make you forget about it,' I said, trying to be understanding.

'Yeah,' he said, but he didn't look as if he believed it too much. 'Let's meet at the Crossroads Filling Station. Tomorrow at noon. How many bullets do you have?'

'A box,' I said. 'Hollow points.'

'I'll bring a box,' he said. 'Hollow points. We'll shoot even-stephen.'

The Crossroads Filling Station was often a meeting place for us. It was a small, tired filling station run by an old man who wasn't much interested in selling gas. He sold worms to passing fishermen and pop to thirsty kids during the summer.

As I said earlier, when David and I saw each other we were by ourselves, alone most of the time. We had a secret friendship:

So the Wind Won't Blow It All Away
Dust . . . American . . . Dust

I was there at the Crossroads Filling Station the next day with my gun and a box of bullets that could have been a hamburger if I had been lucky.

I arrived first and parked my bicycle and went and got a bottle of pop. I had my rifle under my arm. I was twelve years old and nobody paid any attention to a kid with a rifle standing in front of a filling station, drinking a root beer.

Needless to say, America has changed from those days of 1948. If you saw a twelve-year-old kid with a rifle standing in front of a filling station today, you'd call out the National Guard and probably with good provocation. The kid would be standing in the middle of a pile of bodies.

'Why did you shoot all these people?' would be one of the first questions asked after he had been disarmed.

'Because I don't like gym,' would be the answer.

'You mean you shot all these people because you didn't like your gym class?'

'Not exactly.'

'What do you mean, not exactly? What actually do you mean? There are twelve dead people here.'

'McDonald's hasn't been putting enough of their special sauce on my Big Macs.'

'You mean, you shot twelve people dead because you don't like gym? and you haven't been getting enough McDonald's special sauce on your hamburgers?'

The kid would look a little bewildered for the first time after his interlude of carnage and then say, 'You mean, those aren't enough good reasons? How would you like something like that to happen to you? Why don't you put yourself in my shoes?' the kid would say, getting into the back seat of the police car and most likely be on his way to parole eight years and seven months from now.

They'd let him out of prison when he was twenty-one, with a baby face and an asshole three inches wide.

'Going shooting?' the old man said, coming out of the filling station. He was rubbing his hands together because it was a cold, cloudy, damp day. It had rained all night and then stopped at mid-morning, around 9.

Everything smelled of rainy winter.

'Yeah,' I said. 'I'm going to try a little target practice.'

'It's a good day for it,' he said.

I didn't know exactly what he meant by that, but I said yes to humor him. Humored, he went back into the filling station to sit beside a pot-bellied stove and sell a few gallons of gas before dark.

He sold a lot of worms and a lot of pop there in the summer

but because it was February, he would have to wait a few months for the fishing season to start and for it to get hot and pop-drinking weather.

I don't know why people didn't want to buy his gasoline. He had a good location there at the Crossroads. There are a lot of life's mysteries which will always remain unsolved.

He didn't seem to care much, so I guess it was all right with him. Maybe the filling station was just an excuse for him to sell worms. There was a big lake ten miles away and he sold a hell-of-a-lot of worms in the summer because the road to the lake went right past his filling station. They were big worms called night crawlers and he bought them from us kids for a penny apiece.

We'd go out at night and pick them up off lawns using a flashlight to see them. The lawns had to be wet to bring the night crawlers out. Rainy nights were of course the best and freshly watered lawns came in second.

I caught my share of night crawlers and sold them to the old man. I would bring in a bucket of worms and he'd count them out very carefully and then give me a penny for each one. He never paid for them with quarters or fifty-cent pieces or dimes. It was always pennies. He counted out the pennies as carefully as he counted out the night crawlers.

Every day during the spring and summer, there would be kids bringing in worms to be counted and leaving with pennies to be spent. It was very simple, earthy capitalism: What crawled out of the ground soon became an ice-cream cone. Also, the old man never turned away a worm, even when the fishing was slow out at the lake. He could always find room to count another worm and pay a penny for its counting, but most of the time he was very busy selling worms.

Gasoline was another story.

The old man's counting was constantly being interrupted by fishermen wanting to buy worms. He sold the worms in pint cartons with a bit of dirt and some wet moss in the cartons to keep the night crawlers fresh. Each carton contained a dozen worms.

When he was interrupted counting out either worms or pennies, he had a notebook that he wrote your first name down in, along with how many worms you brought in. He would count out all the worms and then count out all the pennies that he owed you.

If he was still counting out your worms when somebody drove up to buy a dozen, he would write down: Jack 18. That meant that he had counted out 18 worms and was still counting.

He would go out and sell some worms and then come back and start with 19. If he had counted out all your worms, say 175, he would write in his book: Jack Total 175, and then he would start counting out your pennies.

If he was interrupted when he was paying you, he would write this down in his notebook: Jack Total 175, 61 paid, and then he'd go out and sell some more worms and come back and start counting again at 62.

Our hands slowly filled up with pennies. They were always freshly minted. He went to the bank and got them. He wouldn't pay us with old pennies.

I don't know.

I think the only reason he had that filling station was that he liked to count worms and pennies. I can't think of another reason.

Can you?

He took care of his worm business in that part of the filling station that used to be the garage. Instead of putting cars up on the rack and finding out what was wrong with their brakes or transmissions or differentials or changing tires or doing anything that would help a car run better, he counted worms and pennies in the garage.

Where there should have been racks of tires, there were long wooden boxes filled with thousands of night crawlers and where there should have been cans of motor oil, there were stacks of pint boxes waiting to be filled with worms.

In his little office in the front, he kept a refrigerator to store the boxes of worms that were ready to sell. He had rigged the refrigerator so that the worms stayed cool in it but wouldn't freeze or suffocate. He called it his worm box. Because he spent so much time in the garage counting, he had a little bell outside the door of the office. There was a sign beside the bell that said: RING FOR WORMS.

Maybe that's why he didn't sell very much gasoline.

It was probably easier for somebody who wanted to buy gas to find a filling station that didn't have a sign out front that said: RING FOR WORMS.

I think a lot of people took advantage of that option because I doubt if he ever sold more than a few gallons a day and that would have been on a good day.

He had a huge cooler just outside of his office where he kept the pop. Every day in the summer he filled the cooler with big blocks of ice and the bottles of pop just floated there in the melting ice, making it the coldest and best-tasting pop in the world. That cooler of pop was a mecca for kids on a hot day. When you couldn't stand the heat any more, you knew that pop was waiting. The old man trusted kids. There was a tin can beside the cooler to put your nickels in or your pennies.

I wish that I could have a bottle of that pop right now.

David pedalled up to the filling station on his bicycle. He had his .22 across the handlebars. Again: it was not an unusual sight back in those days just after the War for kids to casually carry guns around with them.

'Want a pop?' the old man came out of his office and asked David.

'No, I'll wait for summer,' David said.

'OK,' the old man said. 'Suit yourself.'

He went back into the filling station to wait for summer.

We pedalled off toward the old abandoned apple orchard that was about three miles away. The day had grown darker and cloudier, but it wasn't very windy. The air was almost stationary with winter dampness. Everything had a slightly decayed, wet smell to it. This was in Western Oregon where the winters are usually just so much rain, days and days, weeks and weeks, months and months of just so much rain.

'How did you sleep last night?' I asked.

'I had that same dream,' David said. 'But it wasn't so bad. I wasn't afraid this time. I just had it and it went away. I couldn't see it, but I didn't really care.'

'Well, I just dreamt about John Wayne,' I said.

'What about him?' David said.

'Nothing,' I said. 'Just John Wayne doing all the things that he does.'

'Were you in the dream?' David said.

'No.'

'At least I was in my dream,' David said.

'You're lucky,' I said. 'I was just watching it like a movie. I wanted to be in it, but I couldn't get out of my seat. I just had to sit there and watch it. I didn't even have a bag of popcorn.'

There were very poor houses along the road to the orchard. People had built along there, I think, just after the First World War, but for some reason or another, it never really caught on as a place for people to live, so they just gradually moved away until now there were only people living in those houses who were very poor.

They had a lot of broken cars in their front yards that were never going anywhere again. The people just used the parts of those cars to try and put together cars that might work for a while. They were not gigantically successful at doing this.

All of their gardens had been crushed by winter storms and their corn patches were defeated and all akilter.

Sometimes dogs barked at us as we rode by, but the dogs were all so useless that they barely presented a threat. There were kids playing around the houses. The kids all looked defeated and out of kilter, too. Instead of being born, they just could have been ears of corn left over from last autumn's harvest.

Low, flat, gray smoke came from the chimneys of the houses. The smoke had a lot of trouble getting any distance into the air, so it just hung there like strange useless sheets that could have been hanging on an odd clothesline.

A kid about ten years old saw us coming and yelled at us when we pedalled by. 'You sons-of-bitches all have bicycles!' he said. 'I'll have a bicycle someday!'

Soon we had left his voice behind like a voice from a dream dreamt down the road, but I looked back into the dream and I could still see him yelling, but I couldn't hear a word. He was just another kid driven crazy by poverty and his drunken father beating him up all the time and telling him that he'd never amount to anything, that he would end up just like his father, which he would.

The old orchard was back in some hills about half a mile from the main road. We had to take a dirt road to get there. The road was narrow and very muddy and it was hard pedalling. There were no houses along the road. About the only thing there was were some abandoned farming equipment and broken-down fences that would never be repaired again.

The grass was a grayish yellow and had been beaten down by an endless series of hard winter storms that were our fate that autumn and winter.

The clouds were gradually lowering and it looked as if it might start raining any time, but we didn't care because we were Pacific Northwest kids and we were used to getting wet. It didn't bother us much at all. We were both wearing raincoats and rubber boots.

We continued pedalling up the road, slinging mud behind us off our rear wheels. It was very slow going. Sometimes we had to get off our bicycles and push them.

No one had used the road in front of us for a long time, not since hunting season. Then pheasant hunters went up there and banged away, but the season had been over for months now and the road had not been used since then.

At the end of the road was a burnt-down farmhouse and half a barn. One half was still standing and the other half had just collapsed because it was too old to hold hands any longer with the rest of the barn.

'I'm always in my dreams,' David said.

Maybe our friendship was based on the fact that he always told me about his dreams because he was constantly talking about them. They were our chief subject of conversation and he always initiated it.

As we pedalled along, I thought about that. We had known each other since July and I had certainly heard a lot about his dreams, especially the nightmare that he couldn't see.

I guess he never told any of his teammates or his parents about the dreams. I was certain that I was the only person he ever talked to about his dreams. I don't think he even mentioned them to his beautiful girlfriend.

If I had a girlfriend like her, I'd tell her all about my dreams, but maybe the reason I didn't have a girlfriend like her was because my dreams were so boring.

But I'm certain he never told her any of his dreams. I guess their friendship was built on things other than dreams, though as I said earlier, he never mentioned her to me.

Once I asked him about her and he changed the subject to Joe DiMaggio's batting average. I didn't pursue it after that because I had absolutely no interest in Joe DiMaggio's batting average. I was a big fan of Ted Williams.

'You don't seem to be in your dreams,' David said, as we neared the burnt-down old farmhouse.

'I try,' I said.

'I don't even have to try,' he said. 'I'm just automatically there. I have no choice.'

We got off our bicycles.

The first drops of heavy rain started falling, but there was quite a bit of distance between the drops. They were falling very slowly and you could almost walk around them if you were interested in doing that.

The trees in the old apple orchard were filled with rotten apples. We loaded our guns and started banging away. It was a tremendous lot of fun to watch the effect of a bullet hitting a rotten apple. They just simply exploded and the bullet continued on viciously scratching white grooves in the still-living branches of the apple trees.

We both had boxes of hollow points and they could really show an apple who was boss. We shot up about twenty rounds apiece and then David decided to walk down to the other end of the orchard where there were some thick bushes because sometimes pheasants hung out down there. I think he liked shooting in the orchard rather than the garbage dump because he was interested in maybe shooting a pheasant, which he was never able to do.

So he went down to the other end of the orchard to see if he could find one to shoot. I sat down on a huge fallen apple branch and waited for him to come back. I sat there wondering why the people had let the orchard go back to nature.

Maybe when their house burnt down they just didn't care to live there any more because it was a sign of bad memories and the apple orchard was a character in their bad memories.

They weren't even interested in selling apples any more. A lot of bad things happen to people in this life that they just don't want to be reminded of, so they move away and try living someplace else where they can forget unpleasant things like their house burning down, and start all over again and build up some good memories.

The big drops of cold gray rain continued falling all around me and the sky was growing lower and lower. It seemed to want to touch the top of the apple trees like putting a gray tent over them.

I was getting a little wet but it didn't bother me.

I sat there continuing to think about David and our dream friendship.

I wondered how it had all gotten started in the first place. It's not an easy thing for a friendship to be founded on one person telling another person about his dreams, but they were the main ingredients of our friendship, and especially the one dream that baffled him so much, the thing that frightened him, the thing that he could almost see, but not quite.

There was something in his mind that kept it out of arm's reach. Though he tried and tried, he couldn't touch it, so he was constantly telling me all about what was not visible to him.

I was interested but not that interested, though I pretended to be because I wanted his friendship, even if it was based mostly on dreams.

Then I heard his .22 go off.

It snapped me alert and I heard the noise of a pheasant rooster coming my way. The bird sounded like a rusty airplane. The bird was coming right at me. I could see him skimming over the grass toward me.

Involuntarily, I snapped my gun up and got a shot off, quite obviously missing the bird that sailed right on past me, heading toward the burnt-down farmhouse and the collapsed barn.

There was a moment for the sound of the gun to disappear along with the pheasant. Then everything was very quiet, and I could hear the rain falling again, big February drops like small self-contained reservoirs.

The plopping of the rain would cause a beautiful green spring in a few months but I wouldn't be there to see it. I hadn't even stood up when I fired the gun. I just cracked off the shot and I had missed the bird by so much that I didn't even try for a second shot. I just turned my head and watched him disappear down around the collapsed barn.

Realizing that the bird and the accompanying shot had come from the direction David had gone in, I got up and yelled down the orchard, 'You missed him!' I didn't think that he must already have known that because he heard me shoot.

Then I wondered where David was. He should have come back up this way by now. He always liked to get a second shot at a pheasant, so he would have wanted to track it down.

Where was David?

'David!' I yelled. 'It came up this way! It's down by the barn!'

David did not answer.

Normally, he was very enthusiastic about stalking and shooting at pheasants with his .22, though I don't recall him ever having shot one, but he never stopped trying. They were like trying to see his dream.

'David!'

Silence

I started down there through the heavy wet grass. I knew that he couldn't be more than a hundred yards away.

'David!'

More silence

'David!'

Silence growing longer, heavier

'Can you hear me?'

I was almost there now – 'David!' – and then I was there. David was sitting on the ground, holding the upper part of his right leg with both of his hands and there was blood spurting regularly between his fingers.

His face was very pale and his features had a dreamy

expression to them, as if he had just awakened or maybe was falling asleep.

The blood was very red and it just kept coming. He seemed to have an endless supply of it.

'What happened?' I said, bending down to look at all the blood that was now covering the ground. I had never seen so much blood before in my entire life, and I had never seen blood that was so red. It looked like some kind of strange liquid flag on his leg.

'You shot me,' David said.

His voice sounded very far away.

'It doesn't look good.'

I tried to say something but my mouth was completely dry as if it had been suddenly sandblasted.

'I wish it would hurt,' he said. 'But it doesn't hurt. Oh, God, I wish it would hurt.'

The bullet had severed the femoral artery in his right leg.

'If it doesn't start hurting soon, I'm going to die,' David said. Then he kind of rolled very slowly over on his side as if he were falling out of the world's slowest chair. He kept holding his leg that was now just a sea of February orchard blood. He looked up at me with eyes that were disappearing right in front of me. They would be gone in a minute.

'Did I get the pheasant?' he asked.

'No,' my voice blew out of the Sahara. It continued blowing. 'I'm sorry. I didn't see you. I just saw the pheasant coming at me, and I fired. I didn't know where you were.'

'I didn't get it, huh?'

'No.'

'Just as well,' David said. 'You can't eat when you're dead. No good,' he said. '*No good*.' He let go of his leg and rubbed his eyes with his bloody hands as if he were trying to see straight because everything had grown fuzzy. The blood on his face made him look like an Indian.

OH, GOD!

'I'll go and get some help. You'll be all right,' I said. I'd just started to run when he stopped me by saying, 'Do you know that thing in my dreams?'

'Yeah,' I said.

'I'm never going to see it now,' David said:

So the Wind Won't Blow It All Away
Dust . . . American . . . Dust

I was acquitted by the court of any negligence in the shooting. I told exactly what had happened and they believed me. I had no reason to shoot him. I was just supposed to listen to his dreams.

David was buried three days later on Tuesday and all the kids in school stopped talking to me.

He was a very popular boy and they retired his basketball jersey. There was a glass case full of trophies in the front hall of the gym and they put his basketball jersey in the case along with a photograph of him and a brass plaque that told his name and how much he was admired for his sportmanship and academic qualities. The plaque also said that he was born March 12th, 1933, and died February 17th, 1948.

David would have been fifteen in a month.

We were off Welfare and my mother was working now as a waitress. It was a small town and her tips stopped, so . . .

There wasn't much point in us hanging around there any more. I got in half-a-dozen fights at school. They weren't my fault. The only thing that was my fault was that I didn't buy that hamburger. If I had only wanted a hamburger that day, everything would have been completely different. There would be another person still living on the planet and talking about his dreams to me.

My mother kept telling me that it wasn't my fault.

'I should have bought a hamburger,' I said.

She was very patient and didn't ask me what I was talking about.

We had this exchange a dozen or so times.

Finally, she said, 'I don't know what you're talking about.'

'It doesn't make any difference,' I said.

Later on that year, after we had moved, and I had taken up my obsessive search for salvation by trying to find out everything there was to know about the hamburger, my mother said to me one day, right out of the blue, startling me because she hadn't made a single comment about my hamburger research, though she was quite aware that it was going on: 'Maybe you should have bought the hamburger.'

I had never told her about the hamburger decision I had made that led to the box of bullets, so I was surprised even more when she told me that I should have bought the hamburger.

'It's too late now,' I said.

She went into the other room without saying anything.

The next day I brought a complete end to my hamburger research. I took all my notes and interviews and assorted documents down to the river that flowed by the new town we were exiled to and burned them in a picnic stove that was beside a very sad little Oregon zoo that barely had any animals and they were all wet because it was raining again as was the fate of that land.

An extremely wet and skinny-looking coyote stood on the other side of his Cyclone fence in a pathetic little compound and watched me burn too many pieces of paper dealing with the origin, refinement and other possibilities of the hamburger.

When all my papers were finally burned and the ashes stirred into oblivion the coyote walked away.

Leaving the zoo, I passed the cage of a black bear. He had a grizzled face. He was staring at the wet cement floor of his cage. He didn't look up as I walked by. I wonder why I still remember him after all these years. He's probably dead now. Bears don't live forever, but I remember him:

So the Wind Won't Blow It All Away
Dust ... American ... Dust

Well, there you have it and now I have released the two people from their paralyzed photograph of 32 years ago, and their truck filled with furniture is coming down the road toward the pond.

The truck rattled to a stop and they got out. They were not surprised to see me because I was their uninvited houseguest, almost every night.

'Hello,' they both said in very slow unison that sounded as if it had originated quite close to Oklahoma. It was not a big friendly hello nor was it a little unfriendly hello. I just said a simple hello hello. I think they were still making up their minds about me.

I was sort of on probation, but I felt as if I were making some progress toward developing a minor pond comrades-in-catfish friendship with them. I had all summer to get to know them. I would outlast them.

Last week they asked me if I wanted to sit down on their couch with them, though that was very difficult because they both were so big that they practically took up the entire couch themselves. I barely made it on the couch with them like the last final squeeze of toothpaste from a tube.

They were both in their late thirties and over six feet tall and weighed in excess of 250 pounds, and they both wore bib overalls and tennis shoes. I haven't the slightest idea what they did for a living because they never said a single word about what kind of job they did.

I had a feeling whatever they did for a living, they did together. They were the kind of people who looked as if they were never apart. I could see them coming to work together, working together, having lunch together and always wearing the same clothes. Whatever they did required that they wear bib overalls and tennis shoes.

I could see them filling out employment forms.

Under the line that asked about previous experience. They just put down 'bib overalls and tennis shoes.'

I also had a feeling that whatever they did, they came directly from work to the pond. I don't think they changed their clothes because different, but always matching pairs of bibs and tennis shoes were their entire wardrobe.

I could imagine them even having special overalls and tennis shoes for church with the rest of the congregation sitting apart from them.

Well, whatever they did for a living hadn't made them rich

because the furniture on the back of their truck was well-worn and looked as if it had not been very expensive to begin with. It looked like ordinary used furniture or the stuff you'd find in any furnished apartment where the rent was cheap.

Their furniture was a replica of the furniture that I had lived with all my twelve years. New furniture has no character whereas old furniture always has a past. New furniture is always mute, but old furniture can almost talk. You can almost hear it talking about the good times and troubles it's seen. I think there is a Country and Western song about talking furniture, but I can't remember the name.

After their perfunctory hello to me, they took the couch off the truck. They were both so efficient and strong that the couch came off the back of the truck like a ripe banana out of its skin. They carried it over to the pond and put it down very close to the water's edge, so they could fish right off it, but still leaving enough space so as not to get their tennis shoes wet.

Then they went back to the truck and got a big stuffed easy chair. The chair did not match the couch which was an Egyptian-mummy-wrapping beige. The stuffed chair was a blood-fading red.

She took the chair off by herself while he stood there waiting to take something off himself. As soon as the stuffed chair was on its way to join the couch by the pond's edge, he got two end tables off the truck and put them on each side of the couch. By this time she had gone back and gotten a rocking chair and set it up.

Then they took a small wood cookstove off the truck and they began creating a little kitchen in the corner of their living room.

The sun was just setting and the pond was totally calm. I

could see the old man standing on his boat dock across from us watching. He was motionless as they unloaded their furniture. Everything was shadowy on his part of the pond and he was just another shadow textured among thousands of other shadows.

They took a box of food and cooking things off the truck and a small table to use for preparing their evening meal. The man started a fire in the stove. They even brought their own wood. He was very good at starting fires because the stove was hot enough to cook on momentarily.

Redwing blackbirds were standing on the ends of the cattails and making their final night calls, saying things to other birds that would be continued the next morning at dawn.

I heard my first cricket chirp.

That cricket sounded so loud and so good that he could have been a star in a Walt Disney movie. Walt should have sent some scouts out and signed him up.

The man started cooking hamburgers.

They smelled good, but I did not pay the attention to them that I would the following February and the long months that I mulled over hamburgers after the shooting. To me now they were just the good smell of hamburgers cooking.

The woman got three once-electric floor lamps that had now been converted to kerosene use off the truck. The kerosene worked real nice, though of course the lamps were not as bright as they would have been if they used electricity.

There was another interesting thing about those lamps. The people had never bothered to remove the cords. They were still fastened to the lamps. The cords didn't look wrong, but they didn't look right either. I wonder why they didn't take them off.

The woman put a floor lamp next to each end table beside

the couch and lit them. The light from the lamps shined down on the end tables.

Then the woman got a cardboard box off the truck and took two photographs out of the box. They were in large ornate frames. I believe one photograph was of her parents and the other photographs was of his parents. They were very old photographs and tinted in the style of long ago. She put them down on one of the tables.

On the other table she put an old clock that had a heavy somber ticking to it. The clock sounded as if eternity could pull no tricks on it. There was also a small brass figure of a dog beside the clock. The figure looked very old and was a companion and watchdog for the clock.

Did I mention that she put a lace doily on the surface of that table before she put the dog and clock there?

Well, I have now, and there was also a lace doily on the end table that held the photographs of their parents. I might add that their parents were not wearing bib overalls and tennis shoes. They were dressed formally in perhaps the style of the 1890s.

There was another kerosene lamp burning on the worktable beside the stove where the burgers were cooking, but it was a traditional lamp. I mean, it looked like a kerosene lamp.

The man was also boiling some water for Kraft dinner and there was a can of pears on the table.

That was going to be their dinner tonight: 32 years ago.

The smoke rising from the stove sought desperately for a pipe but not finding one just drifted slowly around like an absentminded cripple.

Their living room was now completely set up except that I have forgotten to mention the *National Geographic* magazines that were on both end tables. Sometimes when the fishing was slow they would just read the *National Geographic* while waiting for a bite.

They drank a lot of coffee from a huge metal coffeepot that he was now filling with water from the pond. They also drank the coffee out of metal cups. They put a lot of sugar in their coffee. Every night they used a pound box of sugar. You could almost walk on their coffee. An ant would have been in paradise if it drank coffee.

While they were setting up this living-room ritual of life beside the pond, I sat in some grass nearby, just watching them, saying nothing.

They hardly spoke either and this evening, their conversation was mostly about people who weren't there.

'Father, Bill would have liked this place,' she said.

They always called each other Mother or Father when they called each other anything. They did not spend a lot of time talking to each other. They had spent so much time together that there probably wasn't much more to be said.

'Yes, Mother, he would have been happy here. This is a good pond.'

'I don't know why people have to move all the time, Father.'

'Neither do I, Mother.'

He flipped over a hamburger in the frying pan on the stove.

'Betty Ann moved in 1930,' he said.

'That means Bill must have moved in either 1929 or 1931 because they moved a year apart,' she said.

'I don't know why either of them moved,' he said.

'Well, don't forget: we moved, too,' she said.

'But it was different with us. We had to move,' he said. 'They didn't have to move. They just could have stayed there. They could still be there if they wanted to be,' he said.

She didn't say anything after he said that.

She just busied herself with the living room beside the pond, futzing like women do when they want to think something over and it needs time.

More crickets had joined in with the first cricket, but the new crickets were not star material. They were just ordinary crickets. No one from Hollywood would ever come to Oregon and sign them up.

I could barely see the old man across the pond on his dock staring at us, but he was fading very rapidly away. When night gets started, it just won't stop.

'How's the Kraft dinner?' she asked, sort of absentmindedly.

She had a feather duster in her hand and was dusting off their furniture that had gotten dusty because of the long gray destroyed road that had taken them to this pond in Oregon in late July 1947, the second year after the sky stopped making all that noise from endless flights of bombers and fighter planes passing overhead like the Hit Parade records of World War II, playing too loud on a jukebox that went all the way to the stars.

I was so glad the War was over.

I stared into the silence of the sky that used to be filled with warplanes.

'It's OK,' he said. 'I always thank the Kraft people for inventing Kraft dinner because you never have any trouble cooking it. A lot more things should be like Kraft dinner. Nice and Easy. Take it nice and easy is my motto.'

'I guess it would be just as well if we don't think about Bill and Betty Ann any more,' she replied to his observation about Kraft dinner. 'We're never going to see them again, anyway. We got a postcard from them in 1935. I was happy they got married. We haven't heard a word since. Maybe they went to work in a plant during the War. They could be anywhere now, but I think they would have liked this place.'

The man was dishing up the Kraft dinner and hamburgers. They would have their dinner and then do some fishing. They would eat their dinner off cheap plates on the couch. When they started eating, they never said another word to each other until they were finished.

'Maybe they don't even fish any more,' he said, bringing two plates of food over to the couch where she had just sat down. 'People change. They give up fishing. A lot of people are interested in miniature golf. Maybe Bill and Betty Ann don't feel like fishing any more.'

'I suppose,' she said. 'But we're too big to play miniature golf, not unless they wanted to use us for the course, Father.'

They both laughed and fell silently to eating their hamburgers and Kraft dinner.

I had become so quiet and so small in the grass by the pond that I was barely noticeable, hardly there. I think they had forgotten all about me. I sat there watching their living room shining out of the dark beside the pond. It looked like a fairy tale functioning happily in the post-World War II gothic of America before television crippled the imagination of America and turned people indoors and away from living out their own fantasies with dignity.

In those days people made their own imagination, like homecooking. Now our dreams are just any street in America lined with franchise restaurants. I sometimes think that even our digestion is a soundtrack recorded in Hollywood by the television networks.

Anyway, I just kept getting smaller and smaller beside the pond, more and more unnoticed in the darkening summer grass until I disappeared into the 32 years that have passed since then, leaving me right here, right now.

Because they never spoke during dinner, I think after they finished eating they probably mentioned a little thing about my disappearance.

'Where did that kid go, Mother?'

'I don't know, Father.'

Then they rigged up their fishing poles and got some coffee and just relaxed back on the couch, their fishing lines now quietly in the water and their living room illuminated by kerosene-burning electric floor lamps.

'I don't see him anywhere.'

'I guess he's gone.'

'Maybe he went home.'